BRAIN GA

HORROR MOVIES
Word Search Puzzles

pil

Publications International, Ltd.

Let's get social!
@Publications_International
@PublicationsInternational
@BrainGames.TM
www.pilbooks.com

A SCARY GOOD TIME

Explore the horror history of cinema like never before with **Brain Games® Horror Movies Word Search Puzzles**. Search and solve through classics from Old Hollywood, slashers from the '80s and '90s, and modern-day gems from all over the world. All puzzles include informative text about who made and starred in the film, and a small synopsis of the plot. The puzzles follow the familiar format: Every word listed is contained within the letter grid. Words in the list can be found in a straight line horizontally, vertically, or diagonally, and they may read either forward or backward. If you need a hint, answers are found in the back of the book.

THE CABINET OF DR. CALIGARI

The Cabinet of Dr. Caligari is a 1920 German silent horror film directed by Robert Wiene. It is one of the earliest horror films, and it's a quintessential work of German Expressionist cinema. The film follows an insane hypnotist who uses a brainwashed man with a sleep disorder to commit murders.

ARTHOUSE

ASYLUM

CALIGARI

CESARE

CONRAD VEIDT (actor)

CULT FILM

EXPRESSIONIST

FRANCIS

GERMAN

HYPNOTIST

JANE

ROBERT WIENE (director)

SILENT

SOMNAMBULIST

STABBING

STRAITJACKET

TWIST ENDING

WERNER KRAUSS (actor)

Answers on page 172.

```
Z X P V Y Z T P C E R A S E C T
Z C T J J G S T F A Q R D R E D
M M M I Q N I S E Y L E I K A T
F L F G W I N I S K K I C S N J
H I R N Y B O L J X Z A G E M A
G F I I G B I U I N J Z L A F N
H T W D N A S B U T I I D X R E
Y L N N U T S M I O S B B W N I
P U F E N S E A H S V M A N G O
N C R T W E R N E R K R A U S S
O T A S V T P M H M U L Y S A C
T L N I S G X O K S P L V K J L
I D C W P V E S E S U O H T R A
S F I T X M G E R M A N I Q U S
T T S J T D I E V D A R N O C B
E N E I W T R E B O R H L K T L
```

FRANKENSTEIN

Frankenstein is one of the quintessential monster movies from the "golden age" of Hollywood. Adapted from a 1927 play by Peggy Webling, directed by James Whale, and starring the prolific Boris Karloff as Frankenstein's monster, it is a pre-Code science-fiction horror film about an obsessed scientist (Colin Clive) who digs up corpses to assemble a living being from their body parts. While he does succeed in creating life, it comes at a terrible price to all involved.

BAVARIAN ALPS

BORIS KARLOFF (actor)

COLIN CLIVE (actor)

CORPSE PARTS

FRITZ

GRAVEROBBER

HENRY

HUNCHBACK

ICONIC

JAMES WHALE (director)

LABORATORY

MAE CLARKE (actor)

MARY SHELLEY (1818)

MOB

MONSTER

MURDER

PRE-CODE

SCI-FI

WATCHTOWER

WINDMILL

```
G M I L N V M H M A Y H Z L D U
R A X O K C W U Z R E S F P U R
A E A T C M Q L O Y T F R I T Z
V C C L F B T R R O E Z G C F
E L Y U X S A N A L D I F I C S
R A V C N R E P R O M J Q R E O
O R U G O H E A C W A G M E L H
B K X B X S K E B M R E U W A U
B E A O P S R H O A Y C R O H N
E L H R I P B G M T S M D T W C
R R O R C O I M C K H D E H S H
L C O L I N C L I V E N R C E B
D B A V A R I A N A L P S T M A
L L I M D N I W O S L G C A A C
M O N S T E R A C U E C A W J K
X S V D K N E U I W Y E M O W I
```

Answers on page 172.

FREAKS

Freaks is a 1932 American pre-Code drama horror film produced and directed by Tod Browning. While it was originally a box-office failure and received critical backlash, it received a reappraisal in the 1960s and is now considered a long-forgotten Hollywood classic. The plot centers around a villainous trapeze artist (Olga Baclanova) who joins a group of carnival sideshow performers. She seduces a circus strongman (Henry Victor) to aid her in marrying and murdering a member of the troupe (Harry Earles) in order to gain his inheritance.

BODY HORROR

CARNIVAL SIDESHOW

CLEOPATRA

CONJOINED TWINS

CULT CLASSIC

DRAMA

DWARF

FRIEDA

HANS

HERCULES

HORROR

LEILA HYAMS (actor)

MONSTER

PRE-CODE

TOD BROWNING (director)

TRAPEZE ARTIST

WALLACE FORD (actor)

```
K O Z N G K T C P N V W T Q D T
U Z U R O R R O H Y D O B M Q B
M W A M A R D N O J A H J O G J
U C T G P W Z J S Z Q S E N F W
M I S N G A R O E H X E D S O C
X S M I F L P I L A A D O T R K
E S A N J L R N U B Z I C E P B
K A Y W V A H E C D O S E R J P
D L H O J C O D R U S L R G W S
W C A R K E R T E F P A P G N J
A T L B N F R W H Y R V H A N G
R L I D E O O I Y O P I H D D U
F U E O I R R N N O L N E S A F
I C L T W D M S B Y V R M D Z T
I T S I T R A E Z E P A R T A F
T J L A R T A P O E L C H V A O
```

Answers on page 172.

THE MUMMY

The Mummy is a 1932 American pre-Code supernatural horror film directed by Karl Freund and starring Boris Karloff as the famous Egyptian mummy. The film is about an ancient Egyptian mummy, Imhotep, who is brought to life by a team of archeologists. He proceeds to disguise himself as a modern-day Egyptian with the intention of finding his reincarnated past lover, Anck-es-en-Amon (Zita Johann). While not as popular as its monster movie siblings, *Dracula* and *Frankenstein, The Mummy* was still a success that spawned countless sequels, spinoffs, and remakes.

ANCK-ES-EN-AMON

ARCHEOLOGISTS

BORIS KARLOFF (actor)

CARL LAEMMLE (producer)

CLASSIC MONSTER

EGYPTIAN

EXPEDITION

FRANK

HELEN

IMHOTEP

KARL FREUND (director)

KILLING

MONSTER

PRE-CODE

RESURRECTED

SACRILEGE

SCROLL OF THOTH

SUPERNATURAL

UNIVERSAL

ZITA JOHANN (actor)

```
E A N H H S B M O N S T E R A B
L M O T T K A R L F R E U N D O
M Q I N O X C C B K K N B B R R
M N T O H Q H K R H P R G E K I
E N I M T P G S J I J I T S N S
A A D A F E I S B J L S F X A K
L H E N O T C H K R N E L N R A
L O P E L O C I M O T U G K F R
R J X S L H T A M O D Z X E C L
A A E E O M P C E D O C E R P O
C T H K R I I K I L L I N G J F
H I Y C C S H N A I T P Y G E F
E Z B N S U P E R N A T U R A L
L T F A R C H E O L O G I S T S
E E L D E T C E R R U S E R A Y
N C N A X U N I V E R S A L T G
```

Answers on page 172.

KING KONG

King Kong is a 1933 American pre-Code adventure horror monster film. Directed and produced by Merian C. Cooper and Ernest B. Schoedsack, it showcased state-of-the-art special effects by Willis H. O'Brien. The film is about a giant ape who is captured from Skull Island and attempts to possess a beautiful young woman. It released to rave reviews and is still considered to be one of the greatest horror films of all time.

ADVENTURE

ANN DARROW

APE

BIPLANE

CARL DENHAM

CLASSIC

DINOSAURS

EMPIRE STATE (Building)

GOAT (greatest of all time)

HORROR

JACK DRISCOLL

JUNGLE

KIDNAP

KONG

MONSTER

MOUNTAIN LAIR

NEW YORK CITY

PRE-CODE

REMAKES (in 1976 and 2005)

SKULL ISLAND

SON OF KONG (1933)

```
B E E A C A G X W Z D D P U E U
L E H B S O N O F K O N G R M E
S K U L L I S L A N D I C O P L
B R J V T C J U N T A U E R I G
Y I A N N D A R R O W S Z R R N
T A P D R K G R Q X E Y E O E U
I L E L V P O D L K C C W H S J
C N F D A E V N A D I L A F T T
K I E X G N N M G S E Q Z A A Q
R A D R X S E T S X I N C M T K
O T O Y E R F A U O J L H N E I
Y N C Z F I L R Z R J Z G A X D
W U E I Q C T N T H E Z O Q M N
E O R R E T S N O M C K M I Z A
N M P Q S R U A S O N I D Q X P
L L O C S I R D K C A J W Z A K
```

Answers on page 173.

CREATURE FROM THE BLACK LAGOON

Creature From the Black Lagoon is a 1954 monster horror film. This iconic film follows a group of scientists into the Amazon forest, where they encounter an amphibious humanoid, called the "Gill-Man." The movie was originally filmed for a black-and-white 3D release in the theaters, but since the 3D movie fad of the early '50s had begun to fade by 1954, most audiences watched the film in 2D. The film was re-released in 1975 in full-color 3D.

AMAZON FOREST

AMPHIBIOUS HUMANOID

BLACK-AND-WHITE (3D)

CREATURE FROM THE BLACK (Lagoon)

CRYPTOZOOLOGY

GILL-MAN

HALF FISH

HALF HUMAN

HORROR FILM

ICONIC

JACK ARNOLD (director)

MARINE BIOLOGY

MONSTER MOVIE

RERELEASED (in 1975)

REVENGE OF THE CREATURE (1955)

SCIENTISTS

SEVERAL KILLED

THE CREATURE WALKS (Among Us) (1956)

THREE-D FILM

THREE-D FILM FAD

UNKNOWN CREATURE

WILLIAM ALLAND (producer)

```
I C O N I C C M G N D V R S B K J P P H
J B A T D H G C A G E O E T F C R J U S
H X K F E T B M Q J S D V R D A O V E Y
M M P B L Z L K I A A I E N F L J D X T
O Z T W L L A G S E E O N V J B M O X T
N O H X I U M C A H L N G X K E E T M H
S G R G K M A R C S E A E W H H R M Y E
T Z E D L L Z Y J I R M O Y A T U L B C
E I E N A I O P A F E U F G L M T I L R
R S D A R F N T C F R H T O F O A F A E
M T F L E D F O K L G S H L H R E R C A
O S I L V E O Z A A D U E O U F R O K T
V I L A E E R O R H C O C I M E C R A U
I T M M S R E O N O I I R B A R N R N R
E N F A J H S L O B N B E E N U W O D E
Q E A I O T T O L F P I A N K T O H W W
E I D L J V Z G D T R H T I I A N X H A
J C Z L I P O Y P L R P U R W E K B I L
H S N I Y D X K J X T M R A S R N A T K
T H U W J T Q W M D X A E M V C U I E S
```

Answers on page 173.

LES DIABOLIQUES

Released in the United States as *Diabolique*, *Les Diabolique*s is a 1955 French psychological horror thriller film co-written and directed by Henri-Georges Clouzot. Based on the 1952 novel *She Who Was No More*, the film focuses on a woman (Véra Clouzot) and her husband's mistress (Simone Signoret) who both conspire to murder their partner (Paul Meurisse).

CHRISTINA

CONSPIRE

DELASSALLE

DROWN

FRENCH

HAUNTING

HORROR

MICHEL

MISSING CORPSE

MORBID

MURDER

MYSTERY

NICOLE

PSYCHOLOGICAL

RERELEASED (1995)

SEDATES

SET-UP

THRILLER

WHODUNIT

```
L S P Y H D D A L E H C I M Z L
D M S S X O Y R E T S Y M Z V O
E D D E Y F R Z M O R B I D B X
S N R I D C A R W Q H C N E R F
A D W O G A H R O S Z X R Y Z O
E V V U W L T O L R C K Z U H W
L U A U P N D E L A S S A L L E
E R I P S N O C S O L A G A M V
R S E T U P C P Y G G M Z Z D K
E S P R O C G N I S S I M H X D
R S X W H O D U N I T H C E O Q
D P T I F W W G N I T N U A H D
L X T L P R E D R U M O A L L N
E W P R E L L I R H T H S G A S
M A N I T S I R H C E L O C I N
N R H K W P Q A C V K Q U Q D N
```

Answers on page 173.

INVASION OF THE BODY SNATCHERS

Invasion of the Body Snatchers is a 1978 American science-fiction horror film that was adapted from the 1955 novel *The Body Snatchers* by Jack Finney. In the movie, a gelatinous race of creatures abandon their home planet and come to Earth and establish themselves as pink flower-like pods. A scientist realizes that people are being replaced by emotionless clones of themselves by the gelatinous creatures soon after people encounter these pods. Slowly but surely, the creatures replace more and more of humanity with the emotionless clones of people.

ABANDONED

ADAPTATION

ALIENS

BROOKE ADAMS

DONALD SUTHERLAND

EARTH

EMOTIONLESS CLONES

EXTRATERRESTRIAL (Beings)

FLOWER-LIKE PODS

HORROR FILM

INVASION OF THE BODY (Snatchers)

JEFF GOLDBLUM

LEONARD NIMOY

NOVEL

REPLACING HUMANITY

REPLICAS

SCIENCE-FICTION

SCIENTISTS

THE BODY SNATCHERS

```
X T E X T R A T E R R E S T R I A L Z W
N L S E R E P L I C A S P B V S P I R B
E E C S M G M D H S Y E A B T D N P V J
D O I C U Z V X B C Z M Q S O V A K X B
N N E G L G Q Y C A Y O I P A J L K T I
A A N I B V O T D K U T F S S C I H H S
L R C J D R V C F H N I I Z D X E L E Q
R D E F L R X G J E M O K N O V N H B L
E N F E O T W S I U N N K O P C S O O S
H I I B G A Q C X O O L J I E G L R D M
T M C W F N S N F P A E B T K S R R Y A
U O T T F K H T O B C S G A I A D O S D
S Y I U E V H T A V G S R T L G S R N A
D O O N J E J N R V E C N P R Q C F A E
L L N B B S D R X A X L M A E U O I T K
A K S O K O E V V A E O G D W P X L C O
N F D U N J U B B D L N S A O F M M H O
O Y X E R X Y L T T R E E K L P Z I E R
D G D K X E C Z H H Q S U C F Z Q T R B
R E P L A C I N G H U M A N I T Y U S W
```

Answers on page 173.

THE BLOB

The Blob is an American science-fiction horror film from 1958. After they see a meteorite crash in a nearby field, boyfriend and girlfriend Steve and Jane go to inspect the impact site. A farmer reaches the site first. The farmer pokes the meteorite, which cracks open, exposing a gelatinous blob. As Steve and Jane arrive, they find the blob has attached itself to the farmer so they take him to a doctor. Before any tests can be done, the blob absorbs the farmer and doctor. Steve and Jane run and tell their parents, but unfortunately no one believes them until it's too late. The blob expands and expands throughout the movie, absorbing all that it comes across.

ALIEN LIFEFORM

ALL CONSUMING

EVERGROWING BLOB

EXTRA-TERRESTRIAL (Being)

GELATINOUS BLOB

HORROR FILM

IMPACT SITE

INDEPENDENT FILM

IRVIN YEAWORTH (director)

KAY LINAKER (writer)

MECHANIC SHOP

METEORITE CRASH

PENNSYLVANIA

REPAIR SHOP

SCIENCE-FICTION

SMALL TOWN

STEVE AND JANE

TAKEN TO THE ARCTIC

THE BLOB

```
I P J S A P T P W C Y V N A B X B A E F
S Q J T H I L Z X B F W G O E O D L N M
T C X E W W N Z O R O K L W L T H I D M
W F I P T W B L U T E B J B A A N E C L
L A C E R I B W L C G J S Z I K A N Y I
O D L U N E S L N N Q U D A R E Y L U F
M I T L H C A T I N O E I A T N E I H R
E Q R T C M E W C N K N Q M S T R F B O
T U X V S O O F I A A M E J E O E E S R
E M P D I R N T I V P C N W R T K F T R
O P W O G N A S L C H M J V R H A O E O
R W S R H L Y Y U A T J I W E E N R V H
I Z E Z E S S E N M G I R Q T A I M E Z
T V C G Z N R I A X I M O N A R L D A X
E S I S N N C I D W S E N E R C Y B N G
C D K E L S E I A N O Y G S T T A G D H
R J P B H B F O B P B R P U X I K B J J
A X F O G B R G J Q E T T A E C X Z A K
S I P N G Q U U V L M R F H F H D R N V
H G O M L I F T N E D N E P E D N I E C
```

EYES WITHOUT A FACE

Eyes Without a Face is a 1960 French-language horror film. It stars Pierre Brasseur as a plastic surgeon who's determined to perform a successful face transplant on his disfigured daughter (Édith Scob). He works to accomplish this by kidnapping and stealing the faces of innocent young women who resemble how his daughter used to look. The film had to have some of its original planned gore minimized to clear European censors; despite this, its release still caused controversy.

ACCIDENT

BODY HORROR

CHRISTIANE

CLASSIC

DISFIGURED

DR. GÉNESSIER

EDNA

FACE TRANSPLANT

FRENCH

GEORGES FRANJU

HETEROGRAFT

HORROR

KIDNAP

LOUISE

LURING

MAULING

MEDICAL HORROR

RERELEASED (1986)

STEALING FACES

```
O F F J P M E L U R I N G J R O
I D L A A P C D A F Y Z T B W H
H E N R C M P G N I C Z N O M R
M S O E M E S E O A U R E D C E
J A V I W D T O R L B O D Y L N
D E H S X I E R D Y K R I H A A
D L E S K C A G A V B R C O S I
I E T E I A L E J N V O C R S T
S R E N D L I S A L S H A R I S
F E R E N H N F X O Y P S O C I
I R O G A O G R Y U H B L R J R
G J G P R F A T I I H J A C H
U H R D B R A N N S E V N I N C
R N A T P O C J N E R V B X O T
E L F Y P R E U G N I L U A M U
D B T P W E S M Z C F R E N C H
```

Answers on page 174.

PSYCHO

Psycho is Alfred Hitchcock's classic psychological horror film. Released in 1960, *Psycho* was controversial for its time but still garnered success at the box office. It was lower budget than many of Hitchcock's previous films, but has sustained itself in time as one of Hitchcock's most famous films.

ACADEMY AWARDS

ADAPTATION

ALFRED HITCHCOCK (director)

BEST ART DIRECTION
(Black & White, nominated)

BEST CINEMATOGRAPHY
(Black & White, nominated)

BEST DIRECTOR (nominated)

BEST SUPPORTING (Actress)

CONTROVERSIAL

HORROR FILM

HUGE SUCCESS

ICONIC

JOSEPH STEFANO (writer)

LASTING IMPACT

MOST FAMOUS FILM (Hitchcock's)

MOTHER'S ILLNESS

MURDER-SUICIDE

NORMAN BATES

PSYCHO

PSYCHOLOGICAL

ROBERT BLOCH (original author)

STRYCHNINE POISONING

TAXIDERMIST

```
R C U W A P S Y C H O L O G I C A L H S
O C I N O C I M S I E E N W Y N L B N T
B M F P V W A S J L O I L L K P P O D R
E E Q K Z R I D H H T H S W T P I L T Y
R K S K C B O D E R U E C P U T C C G C
T Y Z T F O E T O M T G M Y C G A E N H
B T M E C O C P C A Y U E E S P U O J N
L L B O I I P H B E R A R S M P I Q O I
O C A I S U N N C D R I W I U T F W S N
C L J I S T A E E T D I G A A C H U E E
H Z L T S M F R M T I N D T R U C L P P
R Q S L R R S A R A I H P T E D D E H O
U E D O G U E A M T T A D M S A S I S I
B X N Y I P T V S O D O L E X E M Y T S
N L V C G S E A O A U N G S R D B S E O
C W I F E J L T N R R S U R E F Y V F N
M D H B L S Z R E Z T N F D A A L Q A I
E M L I F R O R R O H N Y I M P S A N N
S S E N L L I S R E H T O M L Z H M O G
G T S I M R E D I X A T M C D M N Y U V
```

THE BIRDS

The Birds is a horror thriller film produced and directed by Alred Hitchcock. The plot is based upon a 1952 short story by Daphne du Maurier of the same name. For days, people in Bodega Bay, California, are attacked by violent swarms of birds that will peck through boats and houses and fly through windows to attack. *The Birds* was nominated for Best Special Effects at the 36th Academy Awards, but lost to *Cleopatra*.

ACADEMY AWARDS

ADAPTATION

AESTHETICALLY (Significant)

ALFRED HITCHCOCK (director)

ARTISTICALLY (Significant)

BEST SPECIAL EFFECTS

BIRD ATTACKS

BODEGA BAY

CALIFORNIA

CLEOPATRA

DAPHNE DU MAURIER (author)

EVAN HUNTER (writer)

EVENTUAL ESCAPE

HORROR FILM

LIBRARY OF CONGRESS

NATIONAL FILM REGISTRY

NATURAL HORROR

ROD TAYLOR (actor)

SHORT STORY

SWARMS OF BIRDS

THE BIRDS

THRILLER

TIPPI HEDREN (actress)

```
F N B Q O R M U D M F C L E O P A T R A
A A E N A T U R A L H O R R O R G L Y N
Y T S S I F L L O Q A I N R O F I L A C
M I T D S E V E N T U A L E S C A P E R
D O S R S N U Y L L A C I T E H T S E A
D N P A E A L F R E D H I T C H C O C K
A A E W R W A P W T H W R E L L I R H T
P L C A G R R Z N S H R F W C H D S O Q
H F I Y N E T U X T H E W P P H V P R A
N I A M O T I Q M I S O B L I H D M R D
E L L E C N S N B P K J R I U Q Z U O R
D M E D F U T M O P C Y R T R V S T R O
U R F A O H I I S I A P A Z S D C E F D
M E F C Y N C R U H T Z E B Y T S I I T
A G E A R A A P E E T A A W A U O G L A
U I C B A V L J P D A P T J K G P R M Y
R S T G R E L Q Z R D M N P H T E Q Y L
I T S L B Q Y X D E R A G O A U Y D E O
E R D U I S V U M N I Y F P D D T K O R
R Y K Z L B S D R I B F O S M R A W S B
```

Answers on page 174

KWAIDAN

Kwaidan is a 1964 Japanese anthology horror film directed by Masaki Kobayashi and based on stories from Lafcadio Hearn's collections of Japanese folk tales. The film consists of four separate and unrelated stories: "The Black Hair," "The Woman in the Snow," "Hoichi the Earless," and "In a Cup of Tea." The film received critical acclaim, winning Special Jury Prize at the 1965 Cannes Film Festival, and an Academy Award nomination for Best Foreign Language Film.

ANTHOLOGY

BLACK HAIR

BLIND

(In a) CUP OF TEA

DUEL

EARS REMOVED

EX-WIFE

FOLK TALES

GHOST STORIES

HOICHI (the Earless)

HORROR

JAPANESE

MINOKICHI

MOSAKU

RAPID AGING

RED RIBBONS

SANDALS

SNOWSTORM

TEA HOUSE

THREE GHOSTS

TRAPPED

YUKI-ONNA

```
U S X J M P N L A N N O I K U Y
B E U K T R A P P E D Z I J Z O
R L K I S S L A D N A S G X F T
I A A P G L R R Z J T T N C D Q
L T S C Q H E X W I F E I U E P
R K O P K U O Q F Y Y W G P V M
H L M K G H T S Q S A N A O O I
H O R R O R A C T A M W D F M N
S F L E U D G I Q S U U I T E O
S T S O H G E E R H T P P E R K
Y S I J A P A N E S E O A A S I
X O C S N O B B I R D E R D R C
G J A N T H O L O G Y Q K I A H
T E A H O U S E N D N I L B E I
S F C Y D K H O I C H I H B I S
H Y D Y M R O T S W O N S U K Q
```

ROSEMARY'S BABY

Rosemary's Baby is a 1968 American psychological horror film written and directed by Roman Polanski. It was incredibly successful—having been nominated for several Golden Globe Awards and two Academy Awards—and is regarded as one of the greatest horror films of all time. Based on Ira Levin's 1967 novel of the same name, it stars Mia Farrow as a young woman who is preyed upon by a Satanic cult with aims to groom her and her baby to be used in their dark rituals.

ANAGRAM

ANTICHRIST

BABY

BRAMFORD

COVEN

GASLIGHTING

GUY WOODHOUSE

PENDANT

ROSEMARY

SATAN

SATANISTS

SCRATCHES

SUICIDE

TANNIS ROOT

TERRY

THREATEN

```
A Y Y B A B C J V Z K Q U D C G
Y L V A T C P T E H W H E S R S
N P M G R D Q E D I C I U S B F
S U A E S U O H D O O W Y U G S
T E R R Y T S I R H C I T N A B
N T G Y Q Q F E N A O R T X S H
E G A K Z E B R A M F O R D L K
T S N V U T N A D N E P W V I M
A A A I S C Y R A M E S O R G O
E T E R A E B K K W C F N A H N
R A A N T T O O R S I N N A T T
H N J H A U R A J O T M F J I M
T I Z D N J O F F U D K T Q N Q
U S H S C R A T C H E S F J G X
O T F K B S G C X G G J F H L W
X S B Z H G X Z W C O V E N H E
```

Answers on page 175.

NIGHT OF THE LIVING DEAD

Night of the Living Dead is a 1968 American independent horror film directed, photographed, edited, and co-written by George A. Romero. It not only spawned a successful franchise, but it is credited with the creation of the modern-day "zombie" monster. The film follows a group of people (Duane Jones, Judith O'Dea, Karl Hardman, Marilyn Eastman, Kyra Schon, and Keith Wayne) who are trying to survive an apocalypse wherein cannibalistic corpses rise again to terrorize and consume the living.

BARBRA

BEN

BONFIRE

BRAINS

CANNIBALISM

CELLAR

CULT CLASSIC

FLESH EATERS

GHOULS

GORE

INDEPENDENT

JOHNNY

JUDY

MOLOTOVS

ROMERO (director and writer)

VIOLENCE

WALKING DEAD

ZOMBIES

```
I D T T D B B N G Y U F D J T U
M E R I F N O B F L O A N I N B
O E C X S L U O H G E C N L E W
L C A P Q V K M F D N S H B D U
O N M Y L A D Y G C D L J R N J
T E Z K E W T N P I R H O A E O
O L T U E C I N O S O J X I P Z
V O H Z Q K J X L S B P B N E O
S I A F L E S H E A T E R S D M
X V C A N N I B A L I S M C N B
Y P W A J K A K R C M K A R I I
N W M N K U O V B T G Q N A G E
N T E S L D D M R L I J N L O S
H Y X Q J Y Y Y A U X E A L R L
O K B U Z K V H B C B R J E E C
J D O R E M O R B T A G Z C K W
```

Answers on page 175.

THE WICKER MAN

The Wicker Man is a 1973 folk horror film directed by Robin Hardy and written by Anthony Shaffer, based on David Pinner's 1967 novel, *Ritual*. The film follows an investigator looking into the disappearance of a young girl. His investigation leads him to a Hebridean island off the coast of Scotland where a commune of occultists live. Unfortunately for the investigator, the occult rituals and overt paganism he finds so disturbing also cause his untimely demise.

ADAPTATION

ANTHONY SHAFFER (writer)

CELTIC PAGANISM

COMMUNE

DISAPPEARANCE

FOLK HORROR

HEBRIDEAN ISLAND

HORROR FILM

INVESTIGATION

INVESTIGATOR

LORD SUMMERISLE

NOVEL

OCCULT

PAGANISM

RITUAL (novel)

RITUALS

ROBIN HARDY (director)

SCOTLAND

SUMMERISLE

THE WICKER MAN

```
R G F O L K H O R R O R A Y R R B P H A
K Z T R D H E I U L Z E B T S Q A O N Z
K Y D R A H N I B O R E I G W G R T P R
Y C W M N H O W B F I K M R A R H W B Y
I N V E S T I G A T O R C N O O Q M T I
H I F N E W E C R X U R I R N D O N L I
M B W O L K N D W V I S F Y N J A F U N
A J Z I S R P Q I T M I S A X M Y H C V
L X E T I I S M U S L H L U R A I O C E
V J S A R X D A H M A S Q E D M E F O S
E N D T E C L M O F I P K P S G T C S T
L O Z P M H X B F N D C P L A N A C W I
S V Y A M U Q E A K I Y A E Q M D O B G
I E C D U U R E K W K U M B A M D M T A
R L O A S M D S E S T J B W N R Z M W T
E J Q E D I H H R I Y Q V Q S A A U T I
M I K X R J T O R K N L U A X T W N T O
M A P B O K J T T B P Z V U X T T E C N
U Y E B L F X Q S C O T L A N D Y Z J E
S H O C E L T I C P A G A N I S M R R V
```

Answers on page 175

THE EXORCIST

The Exorcist is a 1973 American supernatural horror film directed by William Friedkin from a screenplay by William Peter Blatty. Despite attempts from several cities to have the film banned, it was the first horror film to be nominated for the Academy Award for Best Picture, and it was selected by the Library of Congress to be preserved in the United States National Film Registry. The film follows a mother (Ellen Burstyn) and her efforts to save her young daughter (Linda Blair) from demonic possession.

CHRIS

CRUCIFIX

CULT CLASSIC

DEMON

DENNING

EXORCISM

FATHER DYER

FATHER MERRIN

HEAD BACKWARDS

KARRAS

MEDALLION

NITROGLYCERIN

PRIEST

REGAN

ROMAN RITUAL

SUPERNATURAL

VIOLENT

VOMIT

```
I  X  P  P  D  N  A  G  E  R  F  N  Y  P  G  T
V  Z  A  D  W  Z  V  C  D  X  B  I  N  K  W  D
I  P  W  B  N  X  H  H  E  T  K  R  I  L  N  M
O  M  U  L  O  I  V  R  N  I  A  R  T  U  C  R
L  T  H  A  M  F  R  I  N  E  R  E  R  T  H  F
E  M  B  R  E  I  Z  S  I  I  R  M  O  I  C  A
N  N  M  U  D  C  P  F  N  H  A  R  G  M  U  T
T  F  F  T  N  U  B  T  G  M  S  E  L  O  L  H
R  O  M  A  N  R  I  T  U  A  L  H  Y  V  T  E
B  Q  C  N  I  C  C  O  C  N  N  T  C  D  C  R
U  S  D  R  A  W  K  C  A  B  D  A  E  H  L  D
E  E  N  E  I  Z  Y  Q  Y  M  L  F  R  X  A  Y
H  L  W  P  A  A  T  S  E  I  R  P  I  F  S  E
N  B  D  U  H  G  M  I  G  O  G  S  N  A  S  R
L  P  A  S  L  N  O  I  L  L  A  D  E  M  I  R
U  E  F  L  E  X  O  R  C  I  S  M  R  G  C  A
```

Answers on page 176

THE TEXAS CHAINSAW MASSACRE

The Texas Chainsaw Massacre is a 1974 American horror film produced, co-composed, and directed by Tobe Hooper, who co-wrote it with Kim Henkel. The film follows a group of friends who are attacked by a family of cannibals while taking a road trip through Muerto County, Texas. It spawned the iconic horror character, Leatherface, and it is credited with originating various elements that make up the "slasher" film subgenre.

CANNIBALS

CHAINSAW

CLASSIC

FINAL GIRL

FRANKLIN

GRAVE ROBBER

HORROR

JERRY

KIRK

LEATHERFACE

MEAT HOOK

PAM

POWER TOOLS

SALLY

SLASHER

SLAUGHTERHOUSE

SOUTHERN

```
D Y L A X K G E T C F K A T V H
F L C L P P S S J Y M U I V R O
W L B M D R X U E F V R S R Z R
S A K S A N U O R Q P E U R K Q
H S O L F K I H R Y E B S X K R
O F O A X W R R Y C P B O T O X
R R H B P O W E R T O O L S V S
R A T I C O N T L Z R R F F M O
O N A N L X D H V B Y E J N M U
R K E N A B S G H X Y V H A P T
A L M A S M D U P P J A P U V H
M I X C S L E A T H E R F A C E
J N I H I I U L G J Q G I F J R
Q M Z C C V U S S L A S H E R N
J X S W A S N I A H C F N N C L
Q N O V F I N A L G I R L N G T
```

Answers on page 176.

JAWS

Jaws is a 1975 American thriller film directed by Steven Spielberg. Based on the 1974 novel by Peter Benchley, it stars Roy Scheider, Richard Dreyfuss, and Robert Shaw as a rag-tag team who find themselves trying to save a local community from a vicious, man-eating shark. It has the distinction of being the first major motion picture to be shot on the ocean, leading to a host of problems with their shark animatronics. Despite a myriad of technical issues, it was the highest-grossing film of all time for a few years, and it is preserved in the United States Library of Congress's National Film Registry.

AMITY ISLAND

ANIMATRONIC

BEACH

BOAT

BOUNTY

BRODY

CAGE

EXPLOSION

GREAT WHITE

HARPOON

HOOPER

KILLER

OCEAN

OCEANOGRAPHER

QUINT

SPIELBERG (director)

THRILLER

TIGER SHARK

VAUGHN

```
M T V P W V K D T T N H B K N G
R E P O O H H N H V Y L O I I E
Z V I L F B A A R A T S J L R C
B B P Q V R R L I U N I B L C S
Q T G U K P P S L G U L C E J J
X C E I F H O I L H O G N R K I
G A X N U M O Y E N B A A M L N
R G P T J A N T R L C K R V Q D
E E L T C A N I M A T R O N I C
A V O K N F P M S K L T K Z H K
T Z S O A B E A C H K N J P Y H
W S I J E O T I G E R S H A R K
H A O A C A X U C L W D F S A J
I A N B O T O B R O D Y Z H M B
T F K Q P G S P I E L B E R G M
E R E H P A R G O N A E C O O D
```

Answers on page 176.

THE OMEN

The Omen is a 1976 supernatural horror film directed by Richard Donner and written by David Seltzer. The plot follows a couple who loses their infant in childbirth, but the husband (Gregory Peck) is able to replace it with an orphaned newborn without his wife's (Lee Remick) knowledge. As the child (Harvey Stephens) grows older, frightening and deadly things begin happening around the family as they learn that the child is the prophesized Antichrist.

ANTICHRIST

CEMETERY

(Cannot enter) CHURCH

DAMIEN

FATHER SPILETTO

HANGED

HORROR

INFANTICIDE

JACKAL CARCASS

KATHY

NANNY

ROBERT

ROME

ROTTWEILER

SATAN

SCARES ANIMALS

SUPERNATURAL

```
S U P E R N A T U R A L B L V J
M C L T E D I C I T N A F N I R
T M L S C X Z H P W N H S S X T
R R G I S R H L J U O A F L E S
E O K R S U S O B J Y N E A A S
B T U H R O K R R V X G O M M A
O T T C E M E T E R Y E E I N C
R W O I H X X A Q H O D O N Y R
M E G T N U Z H A S D R Y A R A
V I D N Q A R J K A T H Y S T C
C L J A O N L C B T A F Y E M L
W E E E M O R F H A Y N A R F A
P R G B F I T S A N N Y V A E K
F L X F G A E P A A O C D C O C
G Z O Y Z C Z N N F G I Z S Y A
H F A T H E R S P I L E T T O J
```

Answers on page 176

CARRIE

Carrie is a 1976 American supernatural horror film directed by Brian De Palma. The screenplay, which was adapted from Stephen King's 1974 novel of the same name, was written by Lawrence D. Cohen. The film follows a sixteen-year-old girl (Sissy Spacek) who turns the tables on her cruel and abusive family and peers. *Carrie* remains a huge influence on popular culture, cementing itself as one of the greatest horror films of all time.

ABUSE

BILLY

BULLYING

CARRIE

CHRIS

ELECTROCUTE

FIRE

HORROR

MARGARET

MENSTRUATION

PIG BLOOD

PRAYER CLOSET

PROM

SIN

STEPHEN KING (author)

SUE

SUPERNATURAL

TELEKINESIS

TOMMY

```
Q K T U P M J U G K V S U C V B
Y Z N X R D O O L B G I P O E P
L G I J O M A R G A R E T Z F T
L N S E M F X B B B B F S N M E
I I X T E I R R A C M N O S I L
B K J U P U C Q C H R I S S U E
Z N V C C F R I U T T D L Y R K
T E S O L C R E Y A R P M O M I
A H B R B F X G U C W M R L N N
R P A T S Y I R B L O R C G K E
V E V C U P T R O T O T G D C S
Q T H E Z S C K E H R D S F X I
V S T L N K B U L L Y I N G F S
S U P E R N A T U R A L T J W C
G P M V I W J D B M V B T S Q U
E S U B A Z I H R E M P Y Q O S
```

Answers on page 177.

SUSPIRIA

Suspiria is a 1977 Italian supernatural horror film directed by Dario Argento. The screenplay was written by Argento and Daria Nicolodi, and was partially based on Thomas De Quincey's 1845 essay, "Suspiria de Profundis" ("Sighs from the Depths"). The film is about an American ballet student (Jessica Harper) who discovers that the German dance academy she transferred to is a front for a supernatural conspiracy.

BALLET

BLANC

CONSPIRACY

FINAL GIRL

FRONT

GERMAN SHEPHERD

HANGED

HORROR

IMPALED

INTERCOM

ITALIAN

MAGGOTS

OCCULT

REANIMATION

SHADOW

SKYLIGHT

STABBED

SUPERNATURAL

SUZY

TANNER

WITCH

```
G B I Q Z S R C F L N W F D Q T
P X N M U K D P R C H Y R E J C
A P O B L E H I R S D E O F G S
P Y I K G I G O F U H Q N I I U
Q T T N P L R B N P T D T N I Z
T T A W A R N H E E G S Z M Y
W H M N O C H H K R T M W E P W
O L I H S O S U I N E O O C A A
D F N L T D B T A L C C L L I
A M A P A S O M A T L R C E E Z
H L E M B P Y A L U A E U J D T
S O R X B I C G I R B T L J M A
N E A H E R N G A A A N T D N N
G J V Z D A A O N L W I T C H N
X S W W C C L T H G I L Y K S E
A Q V H B Y B S R J T T X H I R
```

Answers on page 177.

THE HILLS HAVE EYES (1977)

The Hills Have Eyes is a 1977 American horror film written, directed, and edited by Wes Craven. The film follows a suburban American family on a road trip who, after getting stranded in the Nevada desert, are targeted by a family of cannibals. The film's script is based on the story of the Scottish cannibal Sawney Bean, which Craven interpreted as how civilized people could descend into perverse behavior.

ABUSE

ASSAULT

BABY

BOB

BOBBY

BRENDA

CANNIBALS

CARTERS

DESERT

DOUG

ETHEL

FRED

HORROR

LYNNE

MAMA

MARS

MERCURY

PAPA JUPITER

PLUTO

RUBY

WES CRAVEN (director)

```
G L B H Q R K V Y K H S D I T U
R M H O R R O R G X S Z H O U P
C V E A L D S U N R E U V L R L
H T K D V U O C E R U B Y B M U
W X N N V D M T D A E T M Q F T
Z H I E L F R W P Y Z J M U U O
J X T R J A P M A S S A U L T T
B J Q B C P M C P M L J I X K X
G O A Z Z L E N A K A M Y X C T
B F B Z X E R E J M B R Z K A R
T F O B M H C O U A I Y S Z W E
M A B Y Y T U O P M N B X X W S
A D K C D E R F I A N A I M P E
V E S U B A Y D T G A B N R C D
J B B U P X Q W E S C R A V E N
Z O L Y N N E B R U B O P H O G
```

Answers on page 177.

DAWN OF THE DEAD

Dawn of the Dead is a 1978 zombie horror film written, directed, and edited by George A. Romero, and produced by Richard P. Rubinstein. While it is technically a sequel to 1968's *Night of the Living Dead*, it contains none of the characters or settings from it. Following the same premise of corpses rising from the dead to feast on the living, the plot follows a group of survivors as they struggle against the undead horde in a shopping mall.

APOCALYPSE

BIKER GANG

CITY

CULT CLASSIC

ESCAPE

FRAN

HELICOPTER

MALL

NATIONAL GUARD

PETER

PHILADELPHIA

RAGE

REANIMATION

REMAKE (2004)

ROGER

ROMERO (director)

STEPHEN

SURVIVAL

ZOMBIES

```
U M M O N O A Q S E I B M O Z O
R R A I J M A P O C A L Y P S E
I B L M E S C A P E S E L H G E
P J L G N A G R E K I B T E T H
K E H N T H Q P M R V J Z L M E
U R P L R C D H W A O U X I Z B
W E G J I D U I M O M E J C B R
N A T I O N A L G U A R D O S E
R N R G U S G A T S M Y P P T M
E I O N T U N D R C R U V T E A
T M G A U R Q E R O L L B E P K
E A E R G V A L E A M A G R H E
P T R F U I I P P V G E S T E T
Q I T K O V K H W P K E R S N Y
Z O J Y U A B I R Y T I C O I K
M N V X Y L X A M D J A G O V C
```

Answers on page 177

HALLOWEEN

Halloween is a 1978 American independent slasher film directed, co-written, and scored by John Carpenter. Starring Donald Pleasance and Jamie Lee Curtis, it follows the murderous Michael Myers as he terrorizes the teenagers of Haddonfield, Illinois. This film was one of the first to spawn the "final girl" horror film trope wherein the (typically female) main character's friends are murdered one by one until she's the only one remaining who can stop the murderer.

ANNIE

BABYSITTING

CARPENTER (director)

FINAL GIRL

GHOST COSTUME

HADDONFIELD

INDIE FILM

KNIFE

LAURIE

LOOMIS

LYNDA

MICHAEL MYERS

SANITARIUM

SLASHER

STABBING

TEENAGERS

THROAT SLASH

VANISHED

```
R M V H R D Z G B L A V R Y L X
M L Z A M I C H A E L M Y E R S
D I T R Q S X O B H N A A U U F
P F T Y Q A Z S Y R E H S A L S
H E T H R O A T S L A S H N V I
A I R L I G H C I Y T E L O B M
D D B P H N V O T N Y F R G U T
D N T J A I A S T Q D R E I O S
O I E Q N B N T I R A I R U I E
N E E A N B I U N G R A D M B L
F K N A I A S M G U T G O L P O
I N A D E T H E A I N O G Y L Q
E I G N Q S E L N H L Y Q F D Z
L F E Y U C D A Q X M V Z S A C
D E R L R K S R E T N E P R A C
H Q S W L R I G L A N I F W I M
```

Answers on page 178.

ALIEN

Alien is a 1979 science-fiction horror film directed by Ridley Scott and written by Dan O'Bannon. It is the first film of the six-film *Alien* franchise. The film follows the crew of Nostromo, a space tug ship, who encounter a derelict spaceship seemingly abandoned in an uncharted zone. Upon entering the ship, the crew comes up against an aggressive alien species that had been set loose on the ship. The art direction around the alien was conducted by Swiss artist H. R. Giger, who is known for his biomechanical and gothic styles.

ACADEMY AWARDS

ALIEN

ALIEN THREE (1992)

ALIEN VS. PREDATOR (2004)

(Alien vs. Predator:) REQUIEM (2007)

ALIEN: COVENANT (2017)

ALIEN: RESURRECTION (1997)

ALIENS (1986)

BIOMECHANICAL

DAN O'BANNON (writer)

DERELICT SPACESHIP

EXTRATERRESTRIAL

H.R. GIGER

HORROR FILM

NOSTROMO

PREQUELS

PROMETHEUS (2012)

RIDLEY SCOTT (director)

RIPLEY

SCIENCE-FICTION

SEQUELS

SIX-FILM FRANCHISE

UNCHARTED PLANET

XENOMORPH

```
Y C U R L H N A R T S S S E Q U E L S V
I X N E S A T O L N H X S G R M Z R G D
I N C Q I R I V I I O P N L U T U H U K
A N H U X I N R A T E S R E E S I W D R
R O A I F P V R T W C N T O I U K K R G
S I R E I L I N F S V I C R M L Q S M K
D T T M L E D S N S E K F O O O A E I X
R C E K M Y A A Q R N R H E V M N H R X
A E D Y F Z N J J G Q E R Y C E O E I P
W R P N R G O D F I V D I E D N N Q X I
A R L S A D B T I H M J Y L T A E A Y C
Y U A R N Q A W I M M U E C A A Y I N S
M S N A C B N F S U E H T E M O R P C T
E E E R H T N E I L A O U U S X T T G S
D R T V I N O R I D L E Y S C O T T X T
A N V N S G N H Q V R E G I G R H U M E
C E K E E A L I E N V S P R E D A T O R
A I D Z H O R R O R F I L M D X A I Y N
M L D E R E L I C T S P A C E S H I P E
Q A A J Y R J B I O M E C H A N I C A L
```

Answers on page 178.

THE SHINING

The Shining is the quintessential psychological horror film, which set the precedent for many mind-bending horror films for decades to come. Directed and produced by Stanley Kubrick, the film is based off of the 1977 Stephen King novel of the same name. In the film, we see Jack Nicholson's character, Jack Torrance, lose his grip on reality under the influence of supernatural forces in the hotel he and his family are caring for during the off season. Stanley Kubrick and actor Shelley Duvall were nominated for two Golden Raspberry Awards, Worst Director and Worst Actress, nominations that have been proven wrong in time due to the movie's lasting effect on pop culture.

ADAPTATION

AX MURDERER

CARETAKER

GOLDEN RASPBERRY (Awards)

HAUNTED

HORROR MOVIE

ISOLATED

JACK NICHOLSON (actor)

MENTAL BREAK

NOVEL

PSYCHOLOGICAL HORROR

RAZZIES

REDRUM

SHELLEY DUVALL (actress)

STANLEY HOTEL

STANLEY KUBRICK
(director, producer, & co-writer)

STEPHEN KING (author)

THE SHINING

TWIN SISTERS

WORST ACTRESS

WORST DIRECTOR

WRITER

```
R Q Y H L U J Z Y M U R D E R A W Y I P
O O S R W E A C Z R E X Y D E T N U A H
R F Y I R R V R O T C E R I D T S R O W
R C W R L E T O H Y E L N A T S Z E K S
O R M R H K B I N U R M V A P B K A T S
H N H S I A B P G N I K N E H P E T S E
L V J Y R T M A S H T U S U R R Q L E R
A J A W Q E E X H A W H K E B L L M E T
C W A K X R T R V V R H E L I A V R E C
I X I C L A O S X A O N A S V Z E G F A
G N S B K C Q I I R A T E U H D Z I J T
O A O B L N Z T R S N D D D R I N A I S
L V L P D Y I O D E N Y A U L J N Q R R
O R A J O R R C M U E I M P H O P I N O
H A T T J M T K H L H X W W T A G H N W
C B E B O D W M L O A M P T N A N G P G
Y J D V A F B E D M L X A O I P T T X L
S A I L P E H S V G Q S D N F A T I G J
P E O Y E S J T P N I Q O Y Q N Y N O E
D X M K C I R B U K Y E L N A T S G X N
```

Answers on page 178.

AN AMERICAN WEREWOLF IN LONDON

An American Werewolf in London is a 1981 comedic horror film written and directed by John Landis. The movie opens with two American backpackers, David and Jack, being attacked by a werewolf in the English countryside. Jack is killed and David is bitten, which causes him to become a werewolf himself the next full moon. David awakes in the hospital and explains to the police that he and Jack were attacked by a rabid dog. David begins to suffer from hallucinations of an undead Jack, who tells him that they were attacked by a werewolf and that he is now a werewolf as well. After hospitalization, David moves in with the nurse from the hospital. They fall in love, but David soon realizes he can't control himself on full moons, wreaking havoc on the city until he is finally stopped.

ACADEMY AWARD

(American)
WEREWOLF IN PARIS
(sequel)

AN AMERICAN
WEREWOLF IN (London)

BEST MAKEUP

CAN'T CONTROL HIMSELF

COMEDIC

ENGLISH COUNTRYSIDE

FULL MOON

HALLUCINATIONS

HORROR FILM

HOSPITALIZATION

JOHN LANDIS
(writer and director)

LOVE STORY

RABID DOG

RAVING MANIAC

SILVER BULLET

THE MOORS

VIOLENT RAGES

WEREWOLF

WEREWOLF ATTACK

YORKSHIRE

```
A F S P H J A Y Y J C S C F Q M O G F E
A N G E C O F C O K I I B N S R C D D P
U A A P G P S H A L S U D I Z A G I F C
J L C M L A N P V D K W R E I D S I A H
U W S Z E L R E I E E A E N M Y Q N W W
V A P N A R R T Z T P M A R R O T S E C
K A X N O B I T N N A M Y T E C C R X P
Y U D G U I H C I E G L N A O W E G H I
P I F L O E T F A N L U I N W W O Q U U
S U L Q M D L A I N O O T Z O A R L G W
F E E O Z O D V N C W R I L A M R F F A
T M O K W Y A I H I O E F V L T R D Y G
Q R G E A R O S B L C A R I C N I R Q J
S S R T T M I R H A T U F E O W O O V Z
Y E R W X L T I K T R R L O W T G I N P
W L Z I G B M S A S O V M L S O P L V F
J S A N U S Z C E R H L Y E A U L J V T
E F E F E H K R R B L I V J E H B F E W
A X C L O D Y O O U R O R Q I Y H D I C
S Z F W H E H M F K L P J E D B S V K N
```

Answers on page 178

POLTERGEIST

Poltergeist is a 1982 supernatural horror film directed by Tobe Hooper and co-written by Steven Spielberg, Michael Grais, and Mark Victor. The film follows the Freeling Family living in a planned community in California called Cuesta Verde, where they begin to encounter strange happenings in their home after an earthquake. A parapsychologist discovers that the development is built upon an old cemetery and that a portal to the underworld had opened in the children's bedroom closet. They flee as the house collapses on itself.

ABDUCTED DAUGHTER

BEDROOM CLOSET

BUILT ON A CEMETERY

CALIFORNIA

CUESTA VERDE

CURSED LAND

EARTHQUAKE

FREELING FAMILY

HORROR FILM

MARK VICTOR (co-writer)

MICHAEL GRAIS (co-writer)

NEW DEVELOPMENT

PARAPSYCHOLOGIST

PLANNED COMMUNITY

POLTERGEIST

POLTERGEIST II: (The Other Side)

POLTERGEIST III

SPIRITUAL ADVISER

STEVEN SPIELBERG (co-writer)

SUPERNATURAL

TOBE HOOPER (director)

"THEY'RE HERE"

(Portal to the) UNDERWORLD

```
I Z K Z C R K Q T S T E Y T Y R M Q B Y
I T T F M G T C S N Z K T R W E I N F Y
I O S U L U Z S I H M A I E P T V F T L
T B I Z I N E I G H A U N S Z H X A P I
S E E L F D R A O C R Q U I F G I P P M
I H G L R E E R L A K H M V T U I U S A
E O R R O R H G O L V T M D A A T N C F
G O E Z R W E L H I I R O A B D S E L G
R P T M R O R E C F C A C L K D I W Z N
E E L B O R Y A Y O T E D A H E E D C I
T R O L H L E H S R O D E U J T G E U L
L J P W V D H C P N R H N T O C R V R E
O B R V M B T I A I W A N I I U E E S E
P Z T F Q O Y M R A O O A R W D T L E R
Y R E T E M E C A N O T L I U B L O D F
W C G O I Q F G P E G M P P O A O P L K
V D E D R E V A T S E U C S J G P M A Y
Y H S T E V E N S P I E L B E R G E N Y
S U P E R N A T U R A L H M T A S N D M
B R K X Q B E D R O O M C L O S E T B K
```

THE THING

The Thing is a 1982 science-fiction horror film directed by John Carpenter and written by Bill Lancaster. The movie follows a group of scientists in Antarctica who encounter a parasitic extraterrestrial lifeform who can mimic and imitate its victims. Not knowing who is infected by the "Thing," the isolated crew becomes increasingly paranoid of each other. The crew tries to escape, while the Thing tries to reassemble its flying saucer and escape as well.

ADAPTED

ALIEN

ALIEN LIFEFORM

ANTARCTICA

ASSIMILATING

BILL LANCASTER (writer)

CULT CLASSIC

ESCAPE

EXTRATERRESTRIAL

IMITATES

INFECTED

ISOLATED

JOHN CARPENTER (director)

JOHN W. CAMPBELL JR. (author)

KEITH DAVID (actor)

KURT RUSSELL (actor)

MIMIC

PARANOIA

PARASITE

SLED DOG

THE THING

WHO GOES THERE? (novella)

```
Y E B I L L E S S U R T R U K Y M J L V
G Y V O E R E H T S E O G O H W L F O T
J Y E D O G N B A X O A Q O D R G S D M
M O N P A R A N O I A X U D H X E S O H
D I H L A I R T S E R R E T A R T X E A
G Q M N A S S I M I L A T I N G L X J B
Z C R I C E U P J B C A H V F J E O V H
S I B E C A S I S Y N I F R O A H X K K
E S Q W T N R N R T G Y S D O N Z C Q E
T S W C J S E P A W B N E O W U A X L I
A A W L A I A R E P L T I C L D R L U T
T L Y S L I C C A N C W A H A A G W R H
I C P A B T S R N E T M K P T O T B T D
M T U M I A A T F A P E T O D E A E D A
I L Y C S S T N C B L E R D B S H K D V
B U A X I G I J E Y D L E C D M O T O I
C C Y T O X Q L H L P L L E S C A P E D
E K E D W P L P K A S G L I B H D X U V
Z K M S I J I K J D O A L W B P E Q O B
I Q Q D R I N A L I E N L I F E F O R M
```

Answers on page 179.

VIDEODROME

Videodrome is a science-fiction body horror film written and directed by David Cronenberg, and was Cronenberg's first film to gain Hollywood studio backing. The movie follows the CEO of a television station into madness as he falls under the influence of mind-control programming from a snuff-film broadcast signal. The film is an exceptional display of body horror, like most of Cronenberg's films, with heavy techno-surrealist themes. The film stars Debbie Harry of Blondie fame, and the acclaimed James Woods.

BLONDIE

BODY HORROR

BROADCASTING

CULT CLASSIC

DAVID CRONENBERG (writer & director)

DEBBIE HARRY (actress)

HORROR FILM

JAMES WOODS (actor)

MADNESS

MENTAL BREAK

MIND-CONTROL

PROGRAMMING

PROVOCATIVE

SCIENCE-FICTION

SNUFF FILM

TECHNO-SURREALIST

TELEVISION

VIDEODROME

```
J K A E R B L A T N E M N H T S N M R E
T K O I F Y M T Z P U Q I S F G C X V E
X P T L H O P P S T M O K N S B C I I Q
N M U E J X E D W G R T O Z M E T D Y H
H I G Q C S X A E B S X U Q G A N X N D
U N B N J H H P H B Q L L D C O H D A S
P D Z I I Y N G R T B V P O L C E V A S
Z C E W R T Q O X O L I V B T A I M U M
W O H C O E S S S B G O E B Y D W J H N
E N E S R A L A S U R R H H C M N Y O S
M T O N R M N B C P R M A R A T G I A D
O R Q U O C E M M D L R O M A R S F H O
R O O F H U R K F I A N E T M I R N Q O
D L X F Y F Q H F I E O F A V I X Y V W
O Z F F D M A R T N Z P R E L G N L P S
E P D I O M O Q B Y Z X L B S I X G E E
D W K L B R I E O F X E R M U H S L J M
I R Z M R Y R P R B T O J V C Y Y T X A
V S H O J G Z K C I S S A L C T L U C J
W A H B O Q S C I E N C E F I C T I O N
```

Answers on page 179.

A NIGHTMARE ON ELM STREET

A Nightmare on Elm Street is a 1984 supernatural slasher film written and directed by Wes Craven, and it is the first installment of the nine-film *Nightmare on Elm Street* franchise. The movie follows a group of Midwestern teens who fall prey to a mangled man who comes to kill them in their dreams. The teens try to stay awake as long as they can, but when they fall asleep, Freddy Krueger comes for them.

A NIGHTMARE ON ELM (Street) (1984, 2010)

DON'T FALL ASLEEP

DREAM WARRIORS (Part 3, 1987)

FIRST INSTALLMENT

FREDDY KRUEGER

FREDDY VS. JASON (Part 8, 2003)

FREDDY'S DEAD: THE FINAL (Nightmare) (Part 6, 1991)

FREDDY'S REVENGE (Part 2, 1985)

HORROR FILM

JOHNNY DEPP (1984 acting debut)

MIDWESTERN TEENS

NATIONAL FILM REGISTRY

NINE-FILM FRANCHISE

ONE OF THE GREATEST (Horror Films of the Time)

SLASHER FILM

SUPERNATURAL

THE DREAM CHILD (Part 5, 1989)

THE DREAM MASTER (Part 4, 1988)

WES CRAVEN (written and directed)

WES CRAVEN'S NEW (Nightmare) (1994)

```
N A T I O N A L F I L M R E G I S T R Y
M W D F C J E H O R R O R F I L M K F T
L E P O X R M L I F R E H S A L S D R S
N S F S N E V G H F E Z M W R U L A E E
J C R N D T L Q J E S E T R A U A Q D T
E R E E L S F E Y R I J H O N B R D D A
G A D E I A S A W O H V E Y I X U G Y E
N V D T H M R B L A C W M G G R T N S R
E E Y N C M O V M L N E X F H W A O D G
V N K R M A I I Q V A N N H T K N S E E
E J R E A E R H Q M R S N D M B R A A H
R O U T E R R T Y J F N L H A Z E J D T
S H E S R D A K E J M E K E R X P S T F
Y N G E D E W V F I L V P U E D U V H O
D N E W E H M Z P Q I A I K O P S Y E E
D Y R D H T A I G Y F R Q N N U A D F N
E D X I T N E K B A E C S L E C A D I O
R E T M F I R S T I N S T A L L M E N T
F P H X F A D Y M J I E V C M V S R A B
K P S M A Y I L S D N W B R R U T F L B
```

Answers on page 179

THE FLY

The Fly is a 1986 American science-fiction horror film directed and co-written by David Cronenberg. The plot of the film involves a mad scientist (Jeff Goldblum) turning into a monstrous human-fly hybrid after one of his experiments goes horribly wrong. It's up to journalist Ronnie (Geena Davis) and her editor, Stathis (John Getz), to put the monster down.

BARTOK SCIENCE

BE AFRAID (Be Very Afraid)

BRUNDLEFLY

CREATURE

CRONENBERG (director)

FUSED

GEENA DAVIS (actress)

HOUSEFLY

JEFF GOLDBLUM (actor)

JOURNALIST

LABORATORY

MONSTER

MUTILATE

RONNIE

SCI-FI

SCIENTIST

SETH

SYNTHETIC

TELEPODS

ULTIMATE FAMILY

```
A E V C Y G J E M S C I F I M V
Q B C R R R C I T E H T N Y S C
E E A E O E T E L E P O D S B Y
R A A A T B S J Y R M T S I C L
E F H T A N C E R E T S N O M I
G R O U R E I F M F R O F Y E M
E A U R O N E F P I Z T Z X Q A
E I S E B O N G F D S D Z L L F
N D E B A R T O K S C I E N C E
A Z F E L C I L E I N N O R D T
D O L J D N S D D E S U F R B A
A H Y A H O T B L G I Z T P K M
V T K M U T I L A T E A B A B I
I E B C I J O U R N A L I S T T
S S I V O U Y M V S G L P D Q L
E J B R U N D L E F L Y D S K U
```

EVIL DEAD II

Evil Dead II is a 1987 comedy horror film directed by Sam Raimi and co-written with Scott Spiegel. It is a remake of Raimi's 1981 *Evil Dead*, and the second film in the five-film *Evil Dead* franchise. After having received large financial backing after the recommendation of Stephen King, Raimi was encouraged to remake *Evil Dead* before creating its sequel, which would be placed in the Middle Ages. *Evil Dead II* stars Bruce Campbell playing Ash Williams, who goes to enjoy a vacation in the woods with his girlfriend. After Ash plays a found recording of ancient texts called the Necronomicon Ex-Mortis, an evil demon is unleashed and possesses Ash's girlfriend and Ash. Ash's girlfriend dies, and Ash continues to try to evade the demon.

ARMY OF DARKNESS

BRUCE CAMPBELL (actor)

CHAINSAW HAND

COMEDY HORROR

CULT CLASSIC

EVIL DEAD II: DEAD BY DAWN

EVIL SPIRIT

FILM SERIES

INDEPENDENT FILM

LOW BUDGET

NECRONOMICON EXMORTIS

OLDSMOBILE DELTA

POSSESSED

REMAKE

SAM RAIMI (director)

SEQUEL

SEVERED HAND

STEPHEN KING (author; supported project)

THE EVIL DEAD

WITHIN THE WOODS (prequel)

N N E J P T I R I P S L I V E P K K V H
E W C V H L O G N I K N E H P E T S A I
C A I Y S C L T E G D U B W O L S P U N
R D S J E T S E I I P U Z H D Y I E C D
O Y S P V H D N B B Q Z S Y J V C K L E
N B A O E E O S S P N Y X G C K O A J P
O D L S R E O S S W M Y Z H F E M M S E
M A C S E V W T E T V A A R A F E E E N
I E T E D I E G N N J I C A I E D R Q D
C D L S H L H E K U N I I E Y F Y Y U E
O I U S A D T O R S D K T G C F H I E N
N I C E N E N N A B U U D C H U O S L T
E D F D D A I W D Q Q Q O O A P R X Y F
X A N D N D H J F W B D N M H M R B Y I
M E T X V A T X O L P S X Q Q D O Y I L
O D S G N R I R Y C P C P E R Z R E K M
R L Q D Z Y W F M Q P S A M R A I M I Z
T I Z S O R Y H R F I L M S E R I E S W
I V X T Z R Q S A C N Q G H P V U Q G A
S E O L D S M O B I L E D E L T A Y I D

Answers on page 180.

THE LOST BOYS

The Lost Boys is a 1987 American supernatural comedy horror film directed by Joel Schumacher. The plot centers around two teenage brothers who move to the fictional town of Santa Carla, CA, with their divorced mother. While it seems normal on the outside, they soon discover that the town is a haven for vampires. The title is a nod to the Lost Boys from J. M. Barrie's stories about Peter Pan, in that these teenaged vampires—as with Peter Pan's friends—never grow old.

BIKER GANG

BLOOD

COMEDY

DAVID

HALF-VAMPIRE

HEAD VAMPIRE

HOLY WATER

HORROR

LONGBOW

LUCY

MICHAEL

SAM

SANTA CARLA

STAKES

STAR

SUPERNATURAL

VAMPIRES

WATER GUNS

T F G H B C D U W H D L N U P Q
D E K S A N T A C A R L A Y F J
G L I U X R O R R O H F Q Q A C
C K G P J N U F Z I L T Z W N H
Z S H E A D V A M P I R E A Q O
D E A R M C O M E D Y M G T J L
N R L N I E C E D S F N Z E N Y
P I F A C X L S E K A T S R W W
E P V T H H U W P G M F Z G M A
L M A U A R C A R A N O B U O T
J A M R E R Y E S D N V N N K E
R V P A L P K M I A H I Q S D R
L I I L Z I V V O W H M H M O H
N X R W B S A L O N G B O W O I
P Z E M W D Q Y Z F I P M B L X
O L K W A N T G S R A T S E B I

HELLRAISER

Hellraiser is a 1987 supernatural horror film written and directed by horror novelist Clive Barker. The film is Barker's directorial debut and is based on his own 1986 novella *The Hellbound Heart*. The film is the first installment of the *Hellraiser* series, which surrounds the mysteries of a mystical puzzle box that summons a group of trans-dimensional, sadomasochistic beings called the Cenobites. The Cenobites do not distinguish between pleasure and pain and torture everyone who comes into the possession of their puzzle box.

ADAPTATION

CENOBITES

CLIVE BARKER (writer and director)

DIRECTORIAL DEBUT

DOUG BRADLEY (Pinhead actor)

HELLBOUND: HELLRAISER (II) (1988)

HELLRAISER (1987, 2022)

HELLRAISER III: HELL ON (Earth) (1992)

HELLRAISER: BLOODLINE (1996)

HELLRAISER: DEADER (2005)

HELLRAISER: HELLSEEKER (2002)

HELLRAISER: HELLWORLD (2005)

HELLRAISER: INFERNO (2000)

HELLRAISER: JUDGMENT (2018)

(Hellraiser:) REVELATIONS (2011)

HORROR FILM

HORROR NOVELIST

MASOCHISTIC

PINHEAD

REMAKE

SADISTIC

SADOMASOCHISTIC

SUPERNATURAL

THE HELLBOUND HEART (novella)

TRANS-DIMENSIONAL

```
H E L L R A I S E R H E L L S E E K E R
H H E L L B O U N D H E L L R A I S E R
F T M L I F R O R R O H M V V C N U G T
H E L L R A I S E R B L O O D L I N E R
T G E K C S P I N H E A D T Y I L Z V A
U E K A M E R B S R Q Q B M F V A I M E
B C G I N O I T A T P A D A M E L T T H
E Y E L D A R B G U O D H T E B W J H D
D T R A N S D I M E N S I O N A L B E N
L M E R S A D I S T I C L F F R J Q L U
A O C E N O B I T E S M N O K K D X L O
I S U P E R N A T U R A L A G E H X R B
R H O R R O R N O V E L I S T R P E A L
O R E D A E D R E S I A R L L E H R I L
T H W F D F R E V E L A T I O N S U S E
C N O L L E H I I I R E S I A R L L E H
E C I T S I H C O S A M O D A S O O R E
R D L R O W L L E H R E S I A R L L E H
I T N E M G D U J R E S I A R L L E H T
D O N R E F N I R E S I A R L L E H D S
```

CHILD'S PLAY

Child's Play is the first film in the successful American supernatural slasher series by the same name starring the homicidal doll, Chucky (Brad Dourif). Directed by Tom Holland and written by Holland, Don Mancini, and John Lafia, the plot involves a boy (Alex Vincent) and his mother (Catherine Hicks) who are terrorized by a doll that contains the spirit of a serial killer.

ANDY

CHUCKY

CRIMINAL

CULT CLASSIC

DETECTIVE

DOLL

(Start of a) FRANCHISE

GOOD GUY

(Strike the) HEART

HORROR

KILLER

MURDERER

NORRIS

POSSESSED

SLASHER

SUPERNATURAL

TOM HOLLAND (director)

VOODOO

```
E J M T P E T M Z M A K B O U D
Q Q X Q O R R D E G N L D S D E
A F M H A M E Y W N D K F L J S
N E S E D C H U C K Y M X A F S
R V H W N R U O S G S W M S R E
E I G X C I A L L G Z G F H A S
R T Y P G M L W T L L Z S E N S
E C W L S I H L K C A E D R C O
D E V R F N G O F I L N L A H P
R T E V P A H O R M L A D D I C
U E N H S L R V O K T L S C S O
M D O O L J D R X D U V E S E B
E S R R V O O D O O G J Y R I U
C F R R N Y E D A V F U H S X C
L V I O O U L L L O D C Y H G P
W K S R S U P E R N A T U R A L
```

Answers on page 181.

PET SEMATARY

Pet Sematary is a 1989 supernatural horror film directed by Mary Lambert and written by Stephen King, who also wrote the novel of the same name upon which the film is based. The film follows a family who move from Chicago to Maine, where they are told about a pet cemetery (spelled sematary) behind their house. After their cat is run over, they bury it on the grounds only to find that it comes back from the dead with a violent demeanor. After the family's son dies tragically, the father decides to bury his son in the pet cemetery only to find that his son comes back with a bad temper as well.

ADAPTATION

BACK FROM THE DEAD

BAD TEMPER

BEHIND THEIR HOUSE

BURIED IN THE PET (Cemetery)

CHICAGO

HORROR FILM

ILLINOIS

MAINE

MARY LAMBERT

NOVEL

PET SEMATARY

REMADE (in 2019)

RUNOVER CAT

SON DIES

STEPHEN KING

SUPERNATURAL

TRAGIC DEATH

UNDEAD

WORLD FANTASY AWARD (Best Novel)

```
W Z A L O U X U O I G R U I B E H B B Z
C S X T E P E H T N I D E I R U B W E A
I E N W X C H I C A G O D E O L E T Y M
Q I D C O L N O V E L S O X C S U R S D
J D A A D R D S U E U I A W U L A A V A
L N U I M Y L T R P G K M O E T Q G K E
S O U T Y E U D E U B H H P A K G I B D
U S Y P T Y R R F I N R X M H T W C H E
A S Y V H R N R L A I O E R D P R D O H
I V T U V A E L E E N S V H Y N C E R T
A C O E T S I B H P T T M E B K B A R M
J F C U P N I T M E M T A N R M A T O O
P A R G O H D Q P A J E C S A C Q H R R
W A L I S N E I I B L S T I Y M A F F F
L H S D I H B N U R N Y N D P A K T I K
I B W H Y C H F K O S E R X A J W Y L C
Q F E T R G L G L I U E Z A C B K A M A
D B H N V J V B A W N Y I X M O R P R B
L Z A H E D A E D N U G U L K D Q G O D
N F Z C G B F J S E N O I T A T P A D A
```

Answers on page 181.

TREMORS

Tremors is a 1990 American monster comedy horror film directed by Ron Underwood. The film follows two young men (Kevin Bacon and Fred Ward) whose efforts to leave their hometown of Perfection, NV, are cut short when strange tremors caused by giant, murderous, underground worms terrorize the town. The handymen, along with a seismologist (Finn Carter) and an eccentric survivalist couple (Michael Gross and Reba McEntire), fight to save the town and its inhabitants from these flesh-eating monsters.

BURT

COMEDY

DESERT

EARL

EYELESS

GRABOID

HEATHER

HORROR

KEVIN BACON (actor)

MONSTER

PERFECTION

PIPE BOMB

RHONDA

RON UNDERWOOD (director)

SEISMOLOGIST

SURVIVALIST

UNDERGROUND

VAL

```
H A J W K I K Z Q U F A F E L M
H S U R V I V A L I S T Y H L V
N E D L R A E R E H T A E H U B
T I J S W W N C T R E S E D V O
T S O J F J P Y N U R H O N D A
N M U V U K K S D X Y D H O S D
R O N U N D E R W O O D U I S X
P L D V L O R E T S N O M T E L
I O E A I E I H O R R O R C L Q
P G R L F U G W E D Q X B E E V
E I G P P R M X I K J R U F Y Y
B S R B S S R D Z J Z G R R E E
O T O H Y D E M O C Y A T E W S
M V U G R A B O I D R A N P D C
B Z N Q R N O C A B N I V E K S
Z I D H Q C S S P Y C C F D N Z
```

Answers on page 181.

JACOB'S LADDER

Jacob's Ladder is a 1990 American psychological horror film directed by Adrian Lyne and written by Bruce Joel Rubin. The film explores themes of post-war PTSD through the bizarre fragmentary visions and hallucinations that Jacob Singer (Tim Robbins) experiences after the Vietnam War. In the decades since its release, the film has garnered a cult following for its plot and special effects, and it has influenced countless other psychological works, such as the *Silent Hill* video game series.

ADRIAN LYNE (director)

AGGRESSION

CHIROPRACTOR

DANTE'S INFERNO (alternative title)

DEAD

FLASHBACKS

HALLUCINATIONS

INFANTRYMAN

JACOB

LADDER

LOUIS

PSYCHIC

PSYCH. HORROR

PTSD

VIETNAM

VISIONS

WAR

```
G C E T L A A U G I Y N Z G S W
Y W A H A D N O I S S E R G G A
H I Z G A I N F A N T R Y M A N
A S K C A B H S A L F C D A D Q
L S V Y B P Y W T F J L V T E T
L L J V Q S S C B I A T I J A S
U Y A E C J K Y G A C U S B D H
C H I R O P R A C T O R I P V Y
I P S Y C H I C Z H B Y O W H R
N J G D S T P J N Z H H N L X E
A W D R K G Y C T N G O S X A D
T E S R A W Y G K D N Y R E Z D
I A D R I A N L Y N E M C R S A
O N R E F N I S E T N A D W O L
N D I H M S G V M A N T E I V R
S Z F T S F Q H L O U I S S Z P
```

Answers on page 181

IT

It is the title of a miniseries and two-part film adaptation based on the 1986 horror novel of the same title by Stephen King. But *It* is really titled after the story's titular antagonist It, an ancient, trans-dimensional evil being who preys upon children in Derry, Maine. As the story goes, every twenty-seven years, It comes out from the sewers shapeshifted in the disguise of Pennywise the Dancing Clown to lure children for him to eat. It can shapeshift, alter reality, and remain invisible to adults all in order to stoke the worst fears of children not just in Derry, but the world over. With the recent film adaptations, *It* has never been more terrifying.

ANCIENT

CHILDREN

DERRY

EVIL

FILM ADAPTATION

HORROR

IT

LOST INNOCENCE

MAINE

MINISERIES

NOVEL

PENNYWISE

SEWER

SHAPESHIFTER

STEPHEN KING (author)

SUPERNATURAL

TERRIFYING

THE BOWERS GANG

THE DANCING CLOWN

THE LOSERS CLUB

TRANS-DIMENSIONAL

TWENTY-SEVEN YEARS

```
X S R E T F I H S E P A H S B D Z B S R
F W S W L Y F G P V U A P H E Q G T E T
I I P S R A E Y N E V E S Y T N E W T H
L J N D T R N C S E N I A M T F E W R E
M Z H V Q N D O N H A N O Z Q S R J S D
A M I N I S E R I E S I Y E Z X S V Y A
D K S Z F B L I S S C P P W I X F D V N
A B G L Y N S W C T N O N Q I C T W Q C
P U N O O O S L V N E E N M H S H K E I
T L I A B V P L A M A P M N D S E S W N
A C Y G X E H K U R H C H I I Y R S U G
T S F B N L V E Z N U O M E D T Y P T C
I R I L M J L L R P T T R K N S S I S L
O E R E Q I Z D T R W Y A R V K N O D O
N S R E Q J E L H B T M F N O O I A L W
O O E A R R B B G B U Y R V R R E N R N
R L T U R R N G Y I M E Q K A E U S G T
B E O Y O E V I L D Q A W U K G P U Y X
M H U R O I J N K N E R D L I H C U Y K
Y T D T H E B O W E R S G A N G Q Q S Y
```

THE SILENCE OF THE LAMBS

The Silence of the Lambs is a 1991 psychological horror film directed by Jonathan Demme and adapted from the 1988 Thomas Harris novel of the same name. The film follows Clarice, played by Jodie Foster, who is an FBI agent pursuing a serial killer, "Buffalo Bill," who kills and skins his female victims. Clarice seeks the advice of the cannibalistic serial killer and criminal psychologist, Dr. Hannibal Lecter, played by Anthony Hopkins. It was the fifth-highest grossing film of 1991, and won all five of the major categories of the Academy Awards: Best Picture, Best Actor, Best Actress, Best Director, and Best Adapted Screenplay.

ACADEMY AWARDS

ADAPTED

ANTHONY HOPKINS (actor)

BEST ACTOR

BEST ACTRESS

BEST ADAPTED (screenplay)

BEST DIRECTOR

BEST PICTURE

BUFFALO BILL

CANNIBAL

CLARICE

CRIMINAL PSYCHOLOGIST

DR. HANNIBAL LECTER

FBI

FEMALE VICTIMS

FIFTH-HIGHEST GROSSING (of 1991)

INVESTIGATION

JONATHAN DEMME (director)

JODIE FOSTER (actress)

PSYCHOLOGICAL

SERIAL KILLER

THE SILENCE OF THE LAMBS

THOMAS HARRIS (author)

```
B Q G T L P L I D K L D C X K S C O T A
E S N S L Q T B G E A R I S O I N R H A
S M I I I F C E R M C G I R U R M E E C
T I S G B U V S E M I V T E A R I T S A
P T S O O S I T L E G F H T P A P C I N
I C O L L S N A L D O L V S E H N E L N
C I R O A N V D I N L S G O C S R L E I
T V G H F I E A K A O I B F I A O L N B
U E T C F K S P L H H D Y E R M T A C A
R L S Y U P T T A T C S S I A O C B E L
E A E S B O I E I A Y T C D L H E I O K
Z M H P E H G D R N S Z Q O C T R N F T
P E G L H Y A J E O P D C J C O I N T A
G F I A J N T M S J E U Y J T G D A H Q
D Q H N L O I J L T S V N C J H T H E W
V X H I A H O Q P K B U A I I T S R L Q
Z O T M I T N A B V X T D G J Z E D A H
R D F I K N D H F F S R I Z T C B S M K
E C I R P A C A D E M Y A W A R D S B V
R Q F C N S P V B E S T A C T R E S S D
```

CANDYMAN

Candyman is a supernatural horror-slasher film series based on Clive Barker's short story "The Forbidden." The original 1992 film depicts a young graduate student studying urban legends who finds her world turned upside down by the "Candyman" legend. Say his name five times in the mirror, and Candyman, the ghost of an artist and son of a slave, comes to get you with his hook.

ADAPTATION

CABRINI–GREEN

CANDYMAN

CHICAGO

CLIVE BARKER (author)

DAY OF THE DEAD

FAREWELL TO THE FLESH

FIVE TIMES

GHOST OF AN ARTIST

GRADUATE STUDENT

HOOK FOR A HAND

HORROR FILM

SERIES

SHORT STORY

SLASHER

SON OF A SLAVE

SUPERNATURAL

THE FORBIDDEN

URBAN LEGENDS

```
W V J G L Z L L O X F Q Q V S T N Z F K
H W S B R K N L Q C O B D O H T N S A Z
F O V D A A P O A W F N N L S V U I R D
E X O F N I D F I D C O M I M P S D E C
I C C K U E U U H T F R T V E N G N W C
H A K S F I G E A A A R E R D S R M E M
T N Q J C O S E S T A T N H E N F Y L O
H D E A C C R L L N E A P T S H E I L Z
E Y A E T L A A A N T S I A O A F X T Q
F M B H R V I F H U A L T G D R L O O Z
O A W D E G O V R A H B A U O A F S T W
R N K R N T I A E M N C R R D S T K H E
B D N V S X L N H B I D R U G E I K E W
I D U O W V I H I H A O D V K R N I F D
D C H Z Q Q X H R H R X L T L J T L U
D G A M V Y F V P S B U K S E I M V E N
E J I Q Y E Y O Y P L A Q E O F W H S L
N H Y R O T S T R O H S C H R X L B H T
N E V S E R I E S G C F I V E T I M E S
S D A Y O F T H E D E A D I Z L M H W M
```

Answers on page 182

BRAM STOKER'S DRACULA (1992)

Bram Stoker's Dracula is a 1992 gothic horror film directed and produced by Francis Ford Coppola and is based on the 1897 epistolary novel. Featuring a star-studded cast with Gary Oldman as Dracula, Winona Ryder as Mina Harker, Keanu Reeves as Jonathan Harker, and Anthony Hopkins as Professor Van Helsing, the film won three Academy Awards for Best Costume Design, Best Sound Editing, and Best Makeup, while also being nominated for Best Art Direction. The story feels as old as time, and the movie will have a lasting impact for decades to come.

ACADEMY AWARD WINNER

ADAPTATION

ANTHONY HOPKINS (actor)

BEST ART DIRECTION

BEST COSTUME DESIGN

BEST SOUND EDITING

BRAM STOKER'S DRACULA

COMMERCIAL SUCCESS

COUNT DRACULA

CRITICALLY ACCLAIMED

EPISTOLARY NOVEL

FRANCIS FORD COPPOLA
(director and producer)

GARY OLDMAN (actor)

GOTHIC HORROR

KEANU REEVES (actor)

OTTOMAN EMPIRE

PROFESSOR VAN HELSING

ROMANTIC-HORROR

TRANSYLVANIA

VLAD THE IMPALER

WINONA RYDER (actress)

```
W  B  I  D  S  R  X  U  D  O  P  M  B  Q  T  V  T  P  Q  S
F  R  T  E  F  A  L  U  C  A  R  D  T  N  U  O  C  R  C  E
R  A  N  M  L  E  C  C  K  A  D  A  P  T  A  T  I  O  N  Q
A  M  J  I  N  P  R  O  G  C  M  N  T  H  P  V  I  F  E  D
N  S  R  A  G  I  E  M  N  A  V  T  R  N  R  U  N  E  M  Y
C  T  O  L  I  S  R  M  I  D  L  H  A  A  S  L  G  S  L  G
I  O  R  C  S  T  I  E  T  E  A  O  N  M  E  R  Q  S  R  O
S  K  R  C  E  O  P  R  I  M  D  N  S  D  V  R  W  O  E  T
F  E  O  A  D  L  M  C  D  Y  T  Y  Y  L  E  G  D  R  D  H
O  R  H  Y  E  A  E  I  E  A  H  H  L  O  E  Y  Y  V  Y  I
R  S  C  L  M  R  N  A  D  W  E  O  V  Y  R  W  E  A  R  C
D  D  I  L  U  Y  A  L  N  A  I  P  A  R  U  D  S  N  A  H
C  R  T  A  T  N  M  S  U  R  M  K  N  A  N  Y  H  H  N  O
O  A  N  C  S  O  O  U  O  D  P  I  I  G  A  H  W  E  O  R
P  C  A  I  O  V  T  C  S  W  A  N  A  H  E  G  Z  L  N  R
P  U  M  T  C  E  T  C  T  I  L  S  R  I  K  O  A  S  I  O
O  L  O  I  T  L  O  E  S  N  E  O  M  C  H  X  F  I  W  R
L  A  R  R  S  Z  G  S  E  N  R  S  C  T  H  D  Y  N  T  Y
A  M  A  C  E  U  X  S  B  E  Y  L  D  U  U  Z  G  G  P  X
P  C  X  H  B  E  S  T  A  R  T  D  I  R  E  C  T  I  O  N
```

Answers on page 182

THE NIGHTMARE BEFORE CHRISTMAS

The Nightmare Before Christmas is a 1993 American stop-motion animated dark fantasy musical film directed by Henry Selick and produced and conceived by Tim Burton. The famous film composer and Oingo Boingo frontman, Danny Elfman, scored the film and was the singing voice of Jack. The plot follows Jack Skellington, the king of "Halloween Town," who feels disillusioned with Halloween. After discovering "Christmas Town," he schemes to take over the holiday for himself.

ANIMATION

DANNY ELFMAN (composer and singer)

DARK FANTASY

FINKELSTEIN

HALLOWEEN TOWN

HENRY SELICK (director)

IGOR

JACK SKELLINGTON

JACK'S LAMENT

MAYOR

MONSTERS

OOGIE BOOGIE

PUMPKIN KING

RAG DOLL

SALLY

SALLY'S SONG

SANDY CLAWS

STOP-MOTION

TIM BURTON (producer)

TOXICOLOGIST

WHAT'S THIS

```
Z K K R R W B Z D B R M N Q I Y
E I G O O B E I G O O A I L S H
P J Y I O C E J G G R M E A I X
U A N S B C V I E U Y O T L H N
M C O A H O P P Z D P N S L T O
P K I L W E R T I W A S L O S I
K S T L E E N A K F D T E D T T
I L O Y H H Y R K S I E K G A A
N A M S W H L R Y R C R N A H M
K M P S T D A M A S N S I R W I
I E O O Z D A N N Y E L F M A N
N N T N Y S A N D Y C L A W S A
G T S G T S I G O L O C I X O T
H A L L O W E E N T O W N C H M
T I M B U R T O N Y L L A S K M
N O T G N I L L E K S K C A J Y
```

Answers on page 183.

SCREAM

Scream is a 1996 American slasher film directed by Wes Craven and written by Kevin Williamson. Serving as the quintessential slasher and "final girl" film of the '90s, *Scream* stars Neve Campbell as Sidney Prescott, a high school student who is targeted by a serial killer around the anniversary of her mother's murder. Sidney and her friends—along with the help of a local sheriff (David Arquette), and a news reporter (Courteney Cox)—struggle to survive against the violence perpetuated by the costumed serial killer known as "Ghostface."

BILLY

CLASSIC

COTTON

DEWEY

FINAL GIRL

GALE

GHOSTFACE

HANGED

HORROR

KENNY

MAUREEN

RANDY

SIDNEY

SLASHER

STABBED

STU

TATUM

WES CRAVEN (director)

WOODSBORO

I	T	Z	Q	Y	D	H	D	G	G	Y	D	N	A	R	E
T	H	Z	V	G	G	G	M	H	E	Y	R	N	P	E	G
K	O	R	O	B	S	D	O	O	W	V	C	M	X	X	J
N	T	A	T	U	M	D	S	S	E	H	A	N	G	E	D
K	S	F	O	W	A	D	D	T	S	I	S	C	Y	P	U
L	R	I	G	L	A	N	I	F	C	U	R	L	L	A	T
Z	B	G	V	D	R	E	A	A	R	M	B	A	L	Q	S
L	Z	L	N	O	T	R	G	C	A	O	Q	S	I	N	G
F	B	S	R	W	Y	F	A	E	V	S	Q	S	B	O	Q
A	Q	R	L	Y	V	C	L	D	E	I	C	I	N	T	P
H	O	C	Q	A	K	O	E	W	N	D	A	C	E	T	V
H	D	Y	F	V	S	U	N	K	U	N	X	D	E	O	P
W	E	V	H	S	G	H	S	U	Q	E	T	Y	R	C	K
Q	W	K	E	N	N	Y	E	L	V	Y	D	G	U	P	X
W	E	S	R	M	A	N	O	R	U	A	E	F	A	C	X
D	Y	T	G	S	T	A	B	B	E	D	H	J	M	C	V

Answers on page 183.

THE CRAFT

The Craft is an American teen supernatural horror film directed by Andrew Fleming from a screenplay by Fleming and Peter Filardi, and a story by Filardi. It was a surprise hit that has gained a large cult following and is often praised for its feminist messaging. The film follows four outcast teenage girls (Robin Tunney, Fairuza Balk, Neve Campbell, and Rachel True) in Los Angeles who dabble in witchcraft in an effort to improve their lives. However, things quickly go wrong and cause strife within the group.

BINDING SPELL

BONNIE

BULLYING

EARTH DEITY

(Four) ELEMENTS CIRCLE

FIGHT SCENE

HARASSMENT

INVOCATION (of the) SPIRIT

MANON

MURDER

NANCY

POWER-HUNGRY

PSYCH. HOSPITAL

ROCHELLE

SARAH

SPELLS

WITCHES

```
K E N O N A M Q R V R F C E B K
K L B B W E A R T H D E I T Y S
S E R E D R U M J S K P K D P E
O M X A Y C N A N R E H E L S H
T E N G D M A T K M Q L T I B C
I N V O C A T I O N S P I R I T
A T F A E N E C S T H G I F N I
P S Y C H H O S P I T A L Z D W
K C R S J N G N I Y L L U B I W
P I H S A U L S L S L O J F N A
N R W B B X H S J T A T G D G K
A C S L L E P S V E J R I D S A
N L H A R A S S M E N T A Y P D
L E P R O C H E L L E S H H E S
I X B O N N I E C M N B D W L G
A Y H Y R G N U H R E W O P L I
```

Answers on page 183.

THE BLAIR WITCH PROJECT

The Blair Witch Project is a 1999 supernatural horror film that revolutionized the found-footage convention so often utilized by horror movies today. The movie follows three student filmmakers on their search for the urban myth of the Blair Witch in Black Hills near Burkittsville, Maryland. The three trek into the woods to do their research but soon get lost and find themselves in the midst of a horrific environment. They lose their map, but end up finding eerie stick figures and a graveyard filled with cairns. After being terrified at night and losing a member of their team, they stumble upon an abandoned house in the woods, a place you never want to enter when you're filming a horror movie.

ABANDONED HOUSE

BLACK HILLS FOREST

BLAIR WITCH (2016)

BOOK OF SHADOWS: (Blair Witch Two) (2000)

BURKITTSVILLE

CEMETERY

CURSE OF THE BLAIR WITCH (1999)

"DOCUMENTARY"

FOUND FOOTAGE

HORROR MOVIE

LOST IN THE WOODS

LOST MAP

MARYLAND

META

SUPERNATURAL

THE BLAIR WITCH PROJECT (1999)

WITCHCRAFT

YOUNG FILMMAKERS

```
B O O K O F S H A D O W S Y W C H P Q T
N V U G I H K D N A L Y R A M C V O H E
A H E L L I V S T T I K R U B N G E N S
A B A N D O N E D H O U S E T D B J D D
O D T H O R R O R M O V I E G L X O Y V
I F G S H O V R B E R O T D A M O Y M H
C U R S E O F T H E B L A I R W I T C H
X G H Y M R J H V Z Y L R G E L L F Z G
X M C Y R E O C E H O W M H C O F O C M
R C T I H E T F D C I Q T F Q S S U T K
M F I U V M T A S T U N Z C P T A N F B
C O W G D C E C L I Y N R G M T D A P
U D R D E C N H M T L H R N R A V F R F
E P I R N Z P M S E B I Z M C P M O C R
O E A D X R Z O X C C S H L E S G O H P
G H L X O H L K W E X C Q K I X B T C V
G Z B J P B I G C Y D D M Z C C F A T P
E F E A F S U P E R N A T U R A L G I V
T C Y R A T N E M U C O D K E B L E W B
T S R E K A M M L I F G N U O Y F B T F
```

Answers on page 183

THE DEVIL'S BACKBONE

The Devil's Backbone is a 2001 Spanish gothic horror film directed by Guillermo del Toro and written by del Toro, David Muñoz, and Antonio Trashorras. The film follows an orphan (Fernando Tielve) who arrives at an orphanage that is run by Republican loyalists during the Spanish Civil War. He soon learns that the war is the least of his problems—a cache of gold is hidden in the orphanage, causing tension between the adults, and there is a vengeful ghost child haunting the place.

BOMB

CARLOS

CIVIL WAR

DOCTOR

FORCE OF INNOCENCE

GHOST

GOTHIC HORROR

GUILLERMO DEL TORO (director)

JACINTO

JAIME

MURDER

ORPHANAGE

SANTI

SPAIN

SPANISH

T A S F I G T K M E J C F Z D B
G H O S T U Q C X C A Q F O A P
G S P A N I S H Y N C Y E W D E
O Z D E K L B T A E I J W X M N
T T R J J L F L O C N R Z I S O
H Y E C E E C U H O T V A A A H
I J D P D R H S G N O J N U C W
C T R S G M U A P N N T M B F O
H N U F K O J N C I V I L W A R
O I M O X D Z T A F R N P M V P
R A P I I E Z I R O C Z X Y P H
R P H F M L Y H L E P T J A J A
O S E L X T G D O C T O R H A N
R H C U Y O M K S R I I Q Y B A
U U B T Z R F N M O C E U C Y G
F C L D F O P T C F B M O B K E

Answers on page 184.

JEEPERS CREEPERS

Jeepers Creepers is a 2001 horror film written and directed by Victor Salva and takes its name from the 1938 song of the same name. In the movie, we watch as brother and sister Trish and Darry Jenner find several dead bodies in the basement of a church while they are on their way home from college. Upon this discovery, they are then pursued by a demonic serial killer who is set on taking their lives. There is no stopping the "Creeper" and Trish barely escapes with her life.

CREEPER

DEMONIC

FRANCHISE

GINA PHILLIPS (actress)

INTERQUEL

JEEPERS CREEPERS (2001)

JEEPERS CREEPERS THREE (2017)

JEEPERS CREEPERS TWO (2003)

(Jeepers) CREEPERS: REBORN (2022)

JONATHAN BRECK (Creeper actor)

JUSTIN LONG (actor)

PURSUIT

REBOOT

ROADTRIP

SEQUEL

SERIAL KILLER

SLASHER FILM

VICTOR SALVA (writer and director)

F Y J C S V I C T O R S A L V A T L K I
C O T E K C N Y S R R L N P W K L B V E
W N E G E S I R B L E S X Z G T C P W I
O K V L B P D V O U A M G E F R K S R K
S C P J X U E S Q B J S B V E H S K B Y
E E Y Q X N S R G A E T H E R Q G Q C E
R R K V Q Z E E S I L R P E R E B O O T
I B H H V T G P Q C N E S C R N Y W Q R
A N E T N T N E G U R A U R P F Y M X P
L A A I R H O E U N E E P G E P I N X Y
K H F B O B R R R N O L E H R P Y L Y H
I T R E A G N C S E B L Z P I S E Y M B
L A A O D Y L S Y P O Y N C E L U E R B
L N N I T V V R Y Y X Z G I B R L O R U
E O C D R E E E A G M E V J T H S I N C
R J H L I V N P W F Y O I L J S D T P W
P E I C P S C E T I U S R U P Z U F W S
F R S X W P D E M O N I C U L W B J J O
Q E E M N R R J I W F S Z U B D B A G J
E E R H T S R E P E E R C S R E P E E J

Answers on page 184.

28 DAYS LATER

28 Days Later is a 2002 British post-apocalyptic zombie horror film directed by Danny Boyle and written by Alex Garland. Actor Cillian Murphy plays a bike courier who is hospitalized after a car accident. When he awakes from his coma, he finds that he is alone in the hospital, which seems to have been totally abandoned and ravaged. He leaves the hospital to find that London itself seems to have been totally abandoned. Confused, he then comes across humans that are infected by the virus called "Rage," which was unleashed upon humanity from a freed lab chimp twenty-eight days earlier. The movie follows the protagonist in his struggle not to be infected.

(28) **DAYS LATER**

(28) **DAYS LATER: THE**
(Aftermath) (graphic novel)

(28) **WEEKS LATER** (sequel)

ABANDONED HOSPITAL

AGGRESSIVE ZOMBIES

ALEX GARLAND (writer)

ALTERNATE ENDINGS

BIKE COURIER

CILLIAN MURPHY (actor)

CRITICAL ACCLAIM

DANNY BOYLE (director)

DESTROYS HUMANITY

ESCAPED LAB CHIMP

FINANCIAL SUCCESS

(Highly) **INFECTIOUS VIRUS**

HORROR FILM

LOW BUDGET

POST-APOCALYPTIC

THE RAGE

TWENTY-EIGHT DAYS

VIRAL INFECTION

WAKING FROM A COMA

ZOMBIES

```
A S U R I V S U O I T C E F N I R C Y S
L J U E S C A P E D L A B C H I M P H G
E H H T W E N T Y E I G H T D A Y S P N
X H T W A K I N G F R O M A C O M A R I
G H O R R O R F I L M N Y W X I K D U D
A U F I N A N C I A L S U C C E S S M N
R U Y W S Y Y W A N L H O O I S E E N E
L F S E I B M O Z A O M P R O V D R A E
A P I E W O K K T I S M I Y L Y X V I T
N K V K T V O E D A N N Y B O Y L E L A
D M K S V I R A L I N F E C T I O N L N
Y U W L J D A Y S L A T E R T H E Y I R
U Y L A T Z I K T H E R A G E P C S C E
H B Q T S L R E I R U O C E K I B X N T
F B K E K I U T E G D U B W O L P W F L
U D F R M I A L C C A L A C I T I R C A
A G G R E S S I V E Z O M B I E S P Q X
Q O N J Y T I N A M U H S Y O R T S E D
J Y L L A T I P S O H D E N O D N A B A
L K C I T P Y L A C O P A T S O P V H M
```

Answers on page 184.

THE RING

The Ring is a 2002 psychological supernatural horror film directed by Gore Verbinski, remaking Hideo Nakata's 1998 *Ring*, which was adapted from Koji Suzuki's 1991 novel of the same name. The film is one of the most successful horror remakes of all time, and grossed nearly $249 million in box-office sales. *The Ring* follows a journalist, played by Naomi Watts, as she investigates a mysterious videotape that supposedly causes your death seven days after being watched. The journalist watches the tape and begins to experience a series of haunting visions of a young girl that begin to loom over her life.

ADAPTATION

DEATH WITHIN SEVEN DAYS

FINANCIAL SUCCESS

GHOSTS

GORE VERBINSKI (director)

HANS ZIMMER (composer)

HIDEO NAKATA (director of original)

HORROR FILM

INVESTIGATION

JOURNALIST

KOJI SUZUKI (author)

MYSTERIOUS VIDEOTAPE

NAOMI WATTS (actress)

NOVEL

PSYCHOLOGICAL

REMAKE

RING

SCARY

SUPERNATURAL

TERRIFYING VISIONS

THE RING

```
S O E U D H S C Q Y G I N G V Y D L B I
M Y P M Z I N I O C L H T O U Y H X K Q
N W A I O N J V K D G U O E V O V S Y T
M L T D N H E O L Z Z H C S R E N I T E
F A O L N I P X U S M R X R T I L N N R
I R E U R E J Q C R A O O D B S B V L R
N U D L R J V A H Q N R H R W G Q E A I
A T I C W A R E Z T F A E G N I R S C F
N A V O T Y T F S I G V L I M J Q T I Y
C N S I O H R A L N E F C I H C C I G I
I R U K V N E M K R I W A L S I O G O N
A E O U H O M R O A E H V S I T U A L G
L P I Z B I M G I D N K T Y Y L D T O V
S U R U H T I R Q N A O A I X L U I H I
U S E S W A Z G T Z G S E M W B X O C S
C E T I M T S U P G J U U D E H D N Y I
C R S J K P N C C R U E F J I R T V S O
E Y Y O G A A L B Z S S S N E H T A P N
S G M K P D H N A O M I W A T T S J E S
S Y E M U A P R N R F R O D X N S X Q D
```

Answers on page 184

SHAUN OF THE DEAD

Shaun of the Dead is a 2004 zombie comedy film directed by Edgar Wright and written by Wright and Simon Pegg. It acquired a cult following in the decades since release, and it is ranked third on Channel 4's list of the 50 Greatest Comedy Films. The film follows a twenty-nine-year-old electronics salesman (Simon Pegg) and his best friend (Nick Frost) as they try to survive a zombie apocalypse in London.

APOCALYPSE

BARBARA

CRICKET BAT

DAVID

DIANNE

ED

EDGAR WRIGHT (director and writer)

ICE-COLD PINT

LIZ

LONDON

PETE

PHILIP

RECORDS

(You've got) RED (on you)

SHAUN

SHOVEL

SIMON PEGG (writer and actor)

WINCHESTER

ZOMBIES

```
S P S Y D L G T N Z K N E N V I
I Z I L I O H N T R X Q J Q F E
M O K X A N K I T U T N Z D R D
O R M V N D N P A S N U A H S G
N E E C N O L D B E X N R X E A
P T P A E N L L T I Z E M B E R
E S R E J R E O E B L E J S N W
G E E T Q V C K M B S P L D R
G H C R P E O E C O X Y G J E I
M C O Y I F H C I Z L E P K R G
X N R L L Q S I R A H G E A Y H
A I D T I D V Z C A I V R D Q T
G W S N H I V O P O S T Z Z A M
B O E F P V P R V E A N C M R R
Z A G E B A R B A R A J S D V M
T Q T S U D B O N S K K B V Y X
```

Answers on page 185

THE DESCENT

The Descent is a British horror film written and directed by Neil Marshall. The film follows six women along a spelunking adventure into a cave, where they are eventually trapped after a narrow passage collapses behind them. The crew hopes to find an exit and continue further into the cave where they begin to encounter humanoid beings called "crawlers." One by one, they are attacked by the crawlers as they try to escape from the horror they have descended into.

BRITISH FILM

CAVE EXPLORING

CAVE PAINTINGS

CAVE SYSTEM

CAVERNS

CLAUSTROPHOBIC

COLLAPSED CAVE

CRAWLERS

FACE YOUR DEEPEST FEAR

GIRLS TRIP

HORROR FILM

HUMANOID CREATURES

KEPT GOING FORWARD

NEIL MARSHALL (writer and director)

NO WAY OUT

SPELUNKING

THE DESCENT

THE DESCENT PART TWO (2009)

TRAPPED

```
K X K E P T G O I N G F O R W A R D W C
E G S U V Q M E T S Y S E V A C A H G A
L Z E P K U Q B C Z F N S K C J E U W V
O X R C X X Y Q N J H B G K L V F F S E
B W U T A L F Q H R W R N P A A T M L E
G N T Q U V E E X M I I I E U K S D L X
N E A T I O E A V Q Y T T A S T E E A P
I D E P R E Y R A E W I N U T O P C H L
K T R W A A P A N X Q S I O R R E Y S O
N R C T C N P P W S I H A P O U E R R R
U W D H R H K T E O X F P S P B D P A I
L V I E A I O G N X N I E A H P R I M N
E U O D W I G R E E D L V H O E U R L G
P S N E L W S M R E C M A K B I O T I S
S M A S E H Y D P O P S C B I N Y S E H
N X M C R Y S P G Z R E E N C E E L N W
S P U E S R A E N G C F W D U X C R M A
K T H N O R Q F A N S U I V E J A I M X
G C Y T T C X U K U E P B L F H F G P B
I C O L L A P S E D C A V E M Q T L F T
```

Answers on page 185.

SLITHER

Slither is a 2006 science-fiction comedy horror film written and directed by James Gunn. While it was a box office failure, it has become a cult classic, and it was Gunn's directorial debut. It follows a small South Carolina town that becomes invaded by a malevolent alien parasite that transforms its host into a tentacled monster.

ALIEN PARASITE

BILL

BRENDA

COMEDY HORROR

ELIZABETH BANKS (actress)

EXPLOSION

GRANT

GRENADE

JACK

JAMES GUNN (writer and director)

KYLIE

METEORITE

MONSTER

NATHAN FILLION (actor)

SCI-FI

STARLA

TENTACLES

```
A  C  A  Q  P  D  E  T  T  J  C  G  B  E  A
L  L  I  B  I  H  H  Q  H  B  A  Q  U  A  Q  L
I  R  O  R  R  O  H  Y  D  E  M  O  C  Z  T  R
E  G  E  E  D  N  R  T  G  R  E  N  A  D  E  A
N  T  M  N  Y  E  M  T  B  C  S  M  X  T  N  T
P  N  E  D  K  Y  L  I  E  R  G  B  W  O  T  S
A  A  T  A  W  M  A  E  V  M  U  P  W  A  W
R  R  E  Z  R  W  P  W  X  V  N  W  S  U  C  X
A  G  O  K  E  C  R  S  J  P  N  M  D  X  L  U
S  P  R  B  T  F  P  P  C  O  L  S  A  M  E  Y
I  M  I  J  S  E  M  B  Q  I  N  O  O  M  S  B
T  T  T  A  N  Q  L  S  L  L  F  O  S  S  O  L
E  E  E  C  O  I  C  B  B  P  G  I  L  I  A  C
C  D  O  K  M  S  T  T  P  X  M  B  Z  S  O  X
K  E  L  I  Z  A  B  E  T  H  B  A  N  K  S  N
V  N  N  A  T  H  A  N  F  I  L  L  I  O  N  Y
```

Answers on page 185

PARANORMAL ACTIVITY

Paranormal Activity is a supernatural horror film written, directed, and produced by Oren Pelo. The movie was Pelo's first foray into movie making and made a splash on the scene with the movie's found-footage conventions. First released as an independent film, it was picked up by Paramount Pictures and re-released in 2009. The film tells the story of a young couple trying to figure out what is going on in their new home. The couple sets up a camera in their house to document the happenings and the horror then unfolds in front of the camera. First filmed for $15,000 and remade by Paramount for $200,000, the film made $194 million in worldwide box-office sales.

ALTERNATE ENDINGS

DIRECTORIAL DEBUT

EVIL PRESENCE

FOUND FOOTAGE

GHOST STORY

HOME SURVEILLANCE

HORROR FILM

INDEPENDENT FILM

OREN PELO (writer, director, & producer)

OUIJA BOARD

PARAMOUNT

PARANORMAL ACTIVITY

RE-RELEASED

REMADE

SUCCESSFUL FRANCHISE

SUPERNATURAL

WRITTEN AND DIRECTED (Oren Pelo)

```
Z V T U B E D L A I R O T C E R I D N W
U O Z L F O U N D F O O T A G E C Y S R
G O Y Y D E S A E L E R E R R H T U M I
C D N Y B R C O X L S V A J O I C H P T
O W M E U J U V H Q I T I M V C M S Y T
P B B D V R T G R L W X E I E L O G U E
A S D L H X K Z P O V S T S I U H N D N
R P J T P Z V R L T U C S F I Y G I W A
A H U O Y S E E E R A F T J X Y S D M N
M U P M S S P A V L U N A H R K U N L D
O U L I E N N E A L E B A O L G P E I D
U T Y N E L I M F D O Z T L P I E E F I
N L C R J L R R N A B S P L Z D R T R R
T E O Y L O A E R I T A E D G O N A O E
U S L A N N P D B S X D D F L I A N R C
I A N A C E M U O W A O A S U J T R R T
I C R H D R L H O R N F M A V L U E O E
E A I N B F G A Z V H L E L W D R T H D
P S I Y O G I D Q I R S R B D P A L E L
E X X A Q M G E I Y P E M I D E L A J S
```

Answers on page 185.

LET THE RIGHT ONE IN

Let the Right One In is a Swedish romantic horror film directed by Tomas Alfredson and written by John Lindqvist, who also wrote the novel the screenplay was based upon. Released in 2008, the movie takes place in the 1980s in suburban Stockholm where a twelve-year-old boy, Oskar, meets a young pale girl, Eli. Eli acts strange for a child her age and tells Oskar they cannot be friends for unexplained reasons. Despite Eli's insistence, they grow to be close friends, and Oskar soon learns Eli is a vampire and needs to kill to survive.

ADAPTATION

BLACKEBERG

CRITICAL ACCLAIM

FRIENDSHIP

GULDBAGGE AWARDS

HORROR FILM

JOHN LINDQVIST (writer)

LET THE RIGHT ONE IN

NOVEL

RELATIONSHIPS

ROMANTIC

SATURN AWARD
(Best International Film)

SEVERAL AWARDS

STRANGE BOND

SUBURBAN STOCKHOLM

SWEDEN

TOMAS ALFREDSON (director)

TRIBECA FILM FESTIVAL
(Best Narrative Feature)

UNEXPLAINED

VAMPIRE

```
L R S S N Q Z A V Z N R E L E B Y Y T N
M T L D S P I H S N O I T A L E R C V V
L R E P R H V M O M M L I F R O R R O H
O I P I K A T D A W S N I B T U M D A D
H B J H V T W N N L Q J Q E L I E S N L
K E O S D J T A X O U G B S A M I P I M
C C H D S I L V E H B G L L B S R I E F
O A N N C E S E B G M E C Q D T W U N P
T F L E U D V X V L G C G G L T U T O M
S I I I J N Z E Y O A A U N T B Q H T U
N L N R Z R E X R L N C B T A J Q F H A
A M D F E W E X A A U H K D Y R O N G D
B F Q T I B R C P Y L T X E L G T N I A
R E V B Z O I K I L N A Z E B U Q S R P
U S I Q S T P L S U A E W N L E G R E T
B T S Q I J M H D O C I D A T A R Q H A
U I T R D I A J H I S B N E R D U G T T
S V C G A I V P M R X Y Z E W D T G T I
S A T U R N A W A R D G G M D S S R E O
P L V N O S D E R F L A S A M O T I L N
```

Answers on page 186

THIRST

Thirst is a 2009 Korean horror vampire film written, produced, and directed by Park Chan-wook. It has the distinction of being the first Korean feature film made with both Korean and U.S. studio funding and distribution. Based on the 1867 novel by Émile Zola, *Thirst* is about a Catholic priest who is turned into a vampire after a failed medical experiment. While he struggles with his new state and tries to abstain from feeding on live people, he begins an affair with the woman (Kim Ok-bin) married to his childhood friend.

BLOATED CORPSE

BLOOD TRANSFUSION

BURNT

CATHOLIC PRIEST

DRINKS BLOOD

(Conflicting) ETHICS

FATAL DISEASE

HEALER

HEALING BLOOD

HOSPITAL

KOREAN

MURDER

PARK CHAN-WOOK
(director, writer, & producer)

SANG-HYUN

TAE-JU

VACCINE

VAMPIRE

VISIONS

```
H N R C M A I D M U B I K D R R
R Z H E A L I N G B L O O D Y F
E T S E I R P C I L O H T A C K
D P A R K C H A N W O O K U E N
R T G E R I P M A V D F I Y E D
U N U Y H G N A S L T Q L T S R
M L N V G N W I R N R S B A A I
Z E S P R O C D E T A O L B E N
X H T W S C I H T E N O J U S K
I Y A E N I C C A V S V Y R I S
O F I H I Z Y U Y N F I E N D B
G X N H V H J D L A U S B T L L
Z H E A L E R B Q E S I A V A O
P C Z C A T C Z Y R I O S U T O
F X P T Y E O G J O O N G P A D
C H O S P I T A L K N S G Z F K
```

Answers on page 186.

DRAG ME TO HELL

Drag Me to Hell is a supernatural horror film directed and co-written by horror great Sam Raimi (*Evil Dead*, *Evil Dead II*). The movie follows a young banker, Christine Brown, who unfortunately has to deny an elderly Roma woman an extension on her loan. The elderly woman pleads and pleads, but is refused. Christine is cursed by the Roma woman and begins to hallucinate horrible visions. A spiritual adviser tells Christine that the demon Lamia will haunt her for three days before she is dragged to hell by the demon. She does what she can to stop the curse, but the forces at work are too great for her to overcome.

CHRISTINE BROWN

CORPORATISM

CURSED

DEMONS

DRAG ME TO HELL

ELDERLY WOMAN

FOLKLORE

HALLUCINATIONS

HAUNTING

HEX

HORRIBLE VISIONS

LAMIA

LOAN FORGIVENESS

POSSESSION

SAM RAIMI (director)

SPIRITUAL ADVISER

SUPERNATURAL

THREE DAYS

```
K B A E M Y D Q D J S G N I T N U A H F
D M E G V L C Q H P O S S E S S I O N J
T R O F Z E A V J I Q N Q F N L U R S L
X C A R B V L M C A B U T O Q M U O N I
Z U U G T M E D I L B G I X Q J S X O A
R W J R M H O E E A J S A Q B C N N I K
Y R R M S E R Z A R I B O U G B O B T X
W I U S D E T E V V L G R E D V M G A S
K K S B T C D O E P U Y G D F R E S N A
G X D S A J Q L H D F E W R R E D G I M
D L L A K B B X C E A J K O O F E C C R
G K E X B I E R Y O L Y R U M A P E U A
P Y U B R H W E W W K L S Z D A Y M L I
S P I R I T U A L A D V I S E R N D L M
M L O A N F O R G I V E N E S S S J A I
C H R I S T I N E B R O W N X N Y U H H
Y R P J L Y K V F O L K L O R E I H S D
O P U W I T X U D M S I T A R O P R O C
I L L A R U T A N R E P U S B I S P L C
Z Q W L V V G Q S A E N Z G X B D K E S
```

Answers on page 186.

INSIDIOUS

Insidious is a 2010 supernatural horror film directed and co-edited by James Wan, and written by Leigh Whannell. This is the first film in the successful *Insidious* franchise that has earned over $730 million worldwide. The film centers on a married couple (Patrick Wilson and Rose Byrne) whose son, Dalton (Ty Simpkins), falls into a coma that doctors can't explain. When they take the still-comatose boy back home, the family witnesses strange, supernatural phenomena such as Dalton getting up and walking around at night, and a frightening apparition.

ASTRAL PROJECT

BLOODY HANDPRINT

COMA

DALTON

DEMON

FOSTER

FRANCHISE

HORROR

JAMES WAN (director)

JOSH

MYSTERIOUS ENTITY

PARANORMAL

PSYCHIC ELISE

RENAI

SEANCE

SUPERNATURAL

THE FURTHER

TORTURED SPIRITS

YOUNG GHOST

```
T  S  Y  Y  O  U  N  G  G  H  O  S  T  S  K  K
D  L  T  H  V  B  C  F  B  B  W  P  U  T  M  T
S  X  I  W  Q  L  M  B  L  F  H  U  D  I  L  S
U  X  T  R  P  O  R  O  R  R  O  H  F  R  I  M
P  N  N  E  S  O  F  X  V  L  I  F  Y  I  J  P
E  T  E  H  Y  D  A  L  T  O  N  I  P  P  O  A
R  R  S  T  C  Y  E  R  V  C  Q  G  F  S  S  R
N  D  U  R  H  H  C  N  I  H  M  Z  R  D  H  A
A  F  O  U  I  A  N  A  O  N  X  I  A  E  N  N
T  O  I  F  C  N  A  W  Z  N  Q  A  N  R  X  O
U  S  R  E  E  D  E  S  O  O  X  N  C  U  L  R
R  T  E  H  L  P  S  E  V  M  I  E  H  T  V  M
A  E  T  T  I  R  A  M  D  E  O  R  I  R  A  A
L  R  S  E  S  I  X  A  M  D  Z  R  S  O  M  L
F  A  Y  I  E  N  Q  J  R  F  E  D  E  T  O  W
R  Z  M  A  S  T  R  A  L  P  R  O  J  E  C  T
```

Answers on page 186.

THE CABIN IN THE WOODS

The Cabin in the Woods is a 2011 science-fiction comedy horror film directed by Drew Goddard in his directorial debut. It was produced by Joss Whedon, and written by Whedon and Goddard. Starring Kristen Connolly, Chris Hemsworth, Anna Hutchison, Fran Kranz, Jesse Williams, Richard Jenkins, and Bradley Whitford, the film follows a group of college students who find themselves in a cabin that's filled with monsters and being controlled by a group of technicians.

ANCIENT ONES

APOCALYPSE

BUCKNER FAMILY

COMEDY HORROR

CONTROL

CURT

DANA

DECAPITATION

FORCE FIELD

HADLEY

HOLDEN

INCANTATIONS

JULES

MANIPULATION

MARTY

MONSTERS

RITUAL

SCI-FI

SITTERSON

SURVEILLANCE

THE DIRECTOR

UNDERGROUND (Facility)

WEREWOLF

ZOMBIES

```
L D K R S H K D S I J Y Y N J M
I S K O U O R N I M C Y T W T A
E R F T R L O U T T U L R E C N
M E O C V D R O T W R I A S D I
R T R E E R R E H T M M P E P
Q S C R I N O G R L H A S Y C U
J N E I L W H R S A G F C L A L
U O F D L H Y E O U K R I A P A
L M I E A O D D N T K E F C I T
E F E H N M E N A I Y N I O T I
S E L T C H M U Y R Z K X P A O
Z J D S E N O T N E I C N A T N
L O R T N O C F D V B U B T I K
R W E R E W O L F A Y B H C O R
I N C A N T A T I O N S K Z N G
Z O M B I E S Y E L D A H F W B
```

Answers on page 187.

THE CONJURING

The Conjuring is a 2013 American supernatural horror film directed by James Wan and written by Chad Hayes and Carey W. Hayes. It kicked off a franchise of horror films that have been given the moniker of *The Conjuring* Universe. It stars Patrick Wilson and Vera Farmiga as Ed and Lorraine Warren, paranormal investigators who find themselves experiencing increasingly disturbing events at their Rhode Island farmhouse.

BATHSHEBA

CLAIRVOYANT

CURSED ARTIFACTS

DEMONIC SPIRIT

DEMONOLOGISTS

ED

EXORCISM

FRANCHISE

HORROR

INAUGURAL FILM

JAMES WAN (director)

LORRAINE

MEDIUM

MUSIC BOX

POSSESSED DOLL

SPIRIT

SUPERNATURAL

WARRENS

```
M W I L R G V Y N H M L G Z W P
X F N D X T N X S O U A T J G O
S K A P E A B H T R S R O A J S
T U U Z M M M P C R I U H M E S
S E G G E N O Z A O C T V E N E
I S U S X L Y N F R B A I S I S
G I R K O K A U I H O N W W A S
O H A V R X B T T C X R S A R E
L C L N C P E I R S S E I N R D
O N F O I O H R A Q N P V V O D
N A I X S G S I D J O U I Z L O
O R L F M A H P E W Q S F R P L
M F M T X R T S S O D D B K I L
E Z D E C L A I R V O Y A N T T
D A V M U T B M U I D E M I U D
L V O K V K F E C W A R R E N S
```

Answers on page 187.

THE BABADOOK

The Babadook is a 2014 Australian psychological horror film written and directed by Jennifer Kent in her feature directorial debut. Based on her 2005 short film, *Monster*, the film follows a mother (Essie Davis) and her son (Noah Wiseman) who face a humanoid monster in their home that cannot be killed or driven out. Regarding the themes of *The Babadook*, Kent explores the fear of going mad and the challenges of parenting.

ADELAIDE

AMELIA

DARKNESS

DEAD HUSBAND

ERRATIC

GLASS SHARDS (in food)

HALLUCINATIONS

HUMANOID MONSTER

IMAGINARY MONSTER

INSOMNIAC

JENNIFER KENT (writer and director)

(Fear of) MADNESS

POSSESSION

PSYCH. HORROR

SAMUEL

SEIZURE

TALONED FINGERS

TOP HAT

TORMENT

```
B R W H B F H A T Y F C D C O R
H E C A I N M O S N I P I R S X
U T H A L L U C I N A T I O N S
M S V B S N G K G W A C Z F R G
A N T A H P O T O R C O K T O L
N O G O X A R H R B J S V N R A
O M T A L O N E D F I N G E R S
I Y A M E L I A D W N P K K O S
D R D A R K N E S S V V Z R H S
M A E D J X E K W R B Y K E H H
O N L P O S S E S S I O N F C A
N I A M P P E R U Z I E S I Y R
S G I B S S E N D A M Q T N S D
T A D E A D H U S B A N D N P S
E M E U L T O R M E N T O E C Q
R I D R L L E U M A S Z X J X X
```

Answers on page 187.

A GIRL WALKS HOME ALONE AT NIGHT

A Girl Walks Home Alone at Night is a 2014 Persian-language American Western horror film written and directed by Ana Lily Amirpour. Promoted as "the first Iranian vampire Western," it was partially crowdfunded on Indiegogo. Starring Sheila Vand as "the girl," it depicts a lonesome vampire going about her nights in the nearly-abandoned town, Bad City.

ANTIHERO	MURDER
ARASH	PERSIAN
ATTI	ROMANTIC
BAD CITY	SAEED
BAD MEN	SKATEBOARDING
BLOOD SUCKING	THE CAT
CHADOR	THE GIRL
FEMINIST	VAMPIRE
HOSSEIN	WESTERN HORROR

```
V M R J G N V M V O E P G A L S
Q C Y M N E R D M H A D I F H A
C N R K I M V A M P I R E R R E
K B P Q D D T M Y T U Q F O I E
T W T S R A V X T V B P R G Z D
A N S R A B T A R O L R R U T T
C I B O O R R A T J O E E C H S
E E Y M B N J J A H O N D O E I
H S L A E F H C N Y D A R K G N
T S K N T U K R T Q S I U A I I
B O I T A D E I I H U S M R R M
X H T I K T C Y H Q C R K A L E
F D Z C S D U I E S K E A S R F
R F I E A U L Q R T I P T H A S
R I W B S O V F O U N Z Y R C H
C C G R C H A D O R G W P B N T
```

Answers on page 187.

WHAT WE DO IN THE SHADOWS

What We Do in the Shadows is a 2014 New Zealand mockumentary horror comedy written and directed by Jemaine Clement and Taika Waititi. The first installment in the *What We Do in the Shadows* franchise, the film stars Clement and Waititi, along with Jonathan Brugh, Ben Fransham, and Cori Gonzalez-Macuer, as a group of vampire housemates trying to thrive in 21st century Wellington. The film spawned a wildy-successful television series spin-off.

DARK BIDDING

DEACON

HORROR COMEDY

HUMAN FAMILIAR

JEMAINE CLEMENT (writer & director)

LEVITATION

MOCKUMENTARY

NICK

PETYR

SUPERNATURAL

(Not) SWEAR-WOLVES

TAIKA WAITITI (writer & director)

TRANSFORM (into animals)

UNHOLY MASQUERADE

VAMPIRE HUNTER

VAMPIRES

VIAGO

VLADISLAV

WELLINGTON

WEREWOLVES

```
V H U V Z A W R O N M B U I J M
A K N H W Y E A V O H N I T E O
M C H V H D R X G I X O G I M C
P I O A U E E Q N T G T O T A K
I N L L M M W O I A L G L I I U
R G Y S A O O G D T C N R A N M
E S M I N C L A D I A I O W E E
H T A D F R V I I V T L P A C N
U R S A A O E V B E Z L E K L T
N A Q L M R S U K L V E T I E A
T N U V I R K V R R A W Y A M R
E S E V L O W R A E W S R T E Y
R F R Q I H H D D E A C O N N D
U O A O A T P T F J G H X W T W
L R D R R S E R I P M A V G Z D
Z M E N S U P E R N A T U R A L
```

Answers on page 188

THE WITCH

The Witch is a 2015 folk horror film written and directed by Robert Eggers. The film was Eggers's directorial debut and attained critical acclaim. The movie is placed in 1630s New England following a family of English settlers who were recently banished from their Puritan settlement. Having built their own homestead, the family makes do by themselves. But everything takes a turn for the worst when their family's newborn baby is kidnapped by a witch. The witch's dark forces quickly dismantle the family's love and resilience.

ANYA TAYLOR-JOY (actress)

BANISHED

BLACK PHILLIP

CRITICAL ACCLAIM

DARK FORCES

DIRECTORIAL DEBUT

ENGLISH SETTLERS

FOLKLORE

HOMESTEAD

HORROR FILM

INTO THE FOREST

KIDNAPPED BABY

NEW ENGLAND SETTLEMENT

OCCULTISM

PURITANISM

RELIGIOUS FAMILY

ROBERT EGGERS (writer and director)

SUNDANCE FILM FESTIVAL

UNBAPTIZED

WITCH

WITCH'S HOVEL

WITCHCRAFT

```
T U E N G L I S H S E T T L E R S L T K
N N T H X W M Z P G I U L A H D V W U C
E B K C Z I S V I S Z V B V Z O D X B R
M A K T H T I K L G A Q U I X E Q K E I
E P D I V C N F L E N U X T H U Q I D T
L T R W R H A R I B Y D I S M Z T D L I
T I Y T E S T F H S A O I E L F S N A C
T Z F F L H I H P R T N D F I O E A I A
E E U E I O R O K O A W O M F L R P R L
S D T D G V U M C B Y I O L R K O P O A
D U V U I E P E A E L T C I O L F E T C
N A B R O L K S L R O C C F R O E D C C
A C R C U T G T B T R H U E R R R H B E L
L R A K S I J E C E J C L C O E T A R A
G B D V F A M A T G O R T N H D O B I I
N U K Z A O V D I G Y A I A P Q T Y D M
E Y K L M A R Y I E F F S D U V N Y L I
W Y J Z I N V C L R Z T M N R V I Y F C
E L P L L T J I E S A L C U G H F Q B I
N B U Y Y U Y M N S Y Q W S N L B L P R
```

Answers on page 188.

10 CLOVERFIELD LANE

10 Cloverfield Lane is a 2016 American science-fiction horror thriller film directed by Dan Trachtenberg in his directorial debut. Produced by J. J. Abrams and Lindsey Weber, and written by Josh Campbell, Matthew Stuecken, and Damien Chazelle, it is the second film in the *Cloverfield* franchise. The plot follows a young woman (Mary Elizabeth Winstead) who wakes up in an underground bunker with two men (John Goodman and John Gallagher Jr.) who claim that the surface is uninhabitable and taken over by interstellar monsters.

APOCALYPSE

BEN

BLACKOUTS

CREATURE

DAN TRACHTENBERG (director)

HAZMAT SUIT

HOSTAGE

HOWARD

MARTIANS

MASSIVE ATTACK

MICHELLE

MUTILATES

PERCHLORIC ACID

SCI-FI HORROR

TENTACLES

UFO

```
E U A U F R J Y O A D V A T Y I
K S P M I U F G S A O A I D P O
C T O Y Y N W T P Z D U R A E F
A U C R E A T U R E S R O N R U
T O A K J Y H C A T S H R T C R
T K L X Y O M Q A E W D R R H U
A C Y L W E W M L S V D O A L S
E A P W R S Z C R N R X H C O S
V L S R H A A E E A U N I H R R
I B E N H T F L W I U U F T I H
S G K R N Q L O I T T Z I E C O
S C K E R E H O T R Z C C N A S
A Y T S H V C A O A C K S B C T
M P T C Q Y D W T M A S Z E I A
S J I S E T A L I T U M Q R D G
T M K M P X P O W W D Q I G K E
```

THE WAILING

The Wailing is a 2016 South Korean horror film written and directed by Na Hong-jin. The film centers on a policeman (Kwak Do-won) who investigates a series of illnesses that cause its victims to become deranged and violent. While trying to piece together what exactly is happening, he's also trying to save his daughter (Kim Hwan-hee) from succumbing to the horrifying illness.

CRITICAL SUCCESS

DEAD GOAT

DEATH SHRINE

EVIL SPIRIT (Moo-myeong)

EXORCISM

GOKSEONG

ILLNESSES

JONG-GOO

KOREAN HORROR

MYSTERY KILLINGS

NA HONG-JIN (writer & director)

NO NAME

POLICE OFFICER

POSSESSION

REANIMATED CORPSE

RED-EYED DEMON

REMOTE VILLAGE

STABBING

```
E M A N O N J S N A K R S T W N
N X P C S E R G U N N E D M Q I
I N F C S V E N G O A C E P P N
R I M T E I M I N I H I G S L R
H X O A C L O L O S O F N T H O
S S O O C S T L M S N F O A C R
H Q G G U P E I E E G O E B I R
T D G D S I V K D S J E S B L O
A G N A L R I Y D S I C K I L H
E F O E A I L R E O N I O N N N
D V J D C T L E Y P T L G G E A
R E A N I M A T E D C O R P S E
L F K N T B G S D K J P R D S R
R M N P I O E Y E U T I N Q E O
D Y K O R O D M R V H P W J S K
Q L I A C E X Y M S I C R O X E
```

Answers on page 188

RAW

Raw is a 2016 coming-of-age body horror drama written and directed by Julia Ducournau. The film premiered at the 2016 Cannes Film Festival, and was theatrically released a year later in the United States and in France. It was critically acclaimed overall, but it did receive some controversy for its graphic content. *Raw* follows a young woman's (Garance Marillier) first year at veterinary school where she not only tastes meat for the first time, but develops a taste for human flesh.

ADRIEN

ALEXIA

BITE

BODY HORROR

CANNIBALISM

COMING-OF-AGE

DRAMA

EXTREME

FLESH

FRENCH

HAZING

JUSTINE

MEAT

MURDER

VEGETARIAN

VETERINARY SCHOOL

```
H A N O E B P P V Y F R E N C H
C Z C X L I I Q E X J R J X I L
J U S T I N E T T I G B J D U T
H T F P E H D N E G F A P W T V
H O U A W K B U R U Q P X O V W
N S E T D C O M I N G O F A G E
A Z M A P A D V N W T D E C Q F
I Q I E O N Y Z A A M F L E S H
R K F M N N H R Y W Y I O B C
A A B F E I O A Y F T A S R E J
T L N T I B R Z S Y K D B E X N
E E K I R A R I C Q P R J D T O
G X N B D L O N H A D A J R R E
E I Q M A I R G O O X M C U E P
V A X H X S J K O P W A E M M V
Y Z J S F M T X L N P P G U E C
```

Answers on page 189.

TRAIN TO BUSAN

Train to Busan is a 2016 South Korean action horror film directed by Yeon Sang-ho. Based on an original story by Park Joo-suk, it grossed $98.5 million worldwide and has launched a successful franchise. *Train to Busan* primarily takes place on a train from Seoul to Busan, focusing on the drama between the passengers as a zombie apocalypse breaks out.

ACTION HORROR

APOCALYPSE

BASEBALL PLAYER

BETRAYAL

BUSAN

CHEERLEADER

FAST UNDEAD

INFECTION

KOREAN

QUARANTINE

SEOK-WOO

STOWAWAY

SU-AN

TRAIN

TRAPPED

ZOMBIE

```
K E N G B L A J Z F T T S H D Q
R K O K N A D A Q G C J F O T A
E J D W B E T R A Y A L L T B G
Y H A T R A P P E D H R D L R O
A C E N O N S M Y G E A P G F Z
L N D R B I U W H D M F S C V Q
P A N H K A Q U A R A N T I N E
L E U H O R X E I R Y N A S U B
L R T R S T L R O Q X A E I F A
A O S F F R N B T K A W M I Y X
B K A L E K A V Y A W A W O T S
E T F E V Z Y W L J Z O M B I E
S T H E K A E S P Y L A C O P A
A C T I O N H O R R O R G T P X
B L C P P S U A N O O W K O E S
V N O I T C E F N I H J B H K R
```

Answers on page 189.

GET OUT

Get Out is a 2017 psychological horror film written, co-produced, and directed by Jordan Peele. The film was Peele's directorial debut and received wide-spread critical and commercial success. It won Best Original Screenplay at the 90th Academy Awards and was nominated for Best Picture, Best Director, and Best Actor. It follows a young black man as he struggles to keep his freedom and his mind when he uncovers the twisted history of his girlfriend's white family.

ACADEMY AWARDS

ALLISON WILLIAMS (actress)

BEST ACTOR

BEST ORIGINAL (Screenplay) (won)

BEST PICTURE

COMMERCIAL SUCCESS

CRITICALLY ACCLAIMED

DANIEL KALUUYA (actor)

DARK HISTORY

DIRECTORIAL DEBUT

FAMILY SECRETS

GET OUT

HORROR FILM

HYPNOTHERAPY

JORDAN PEELE (writer and director)

LAKEITH STANFIELD

MICHAEL ABELS (composer)

PSYCHOLOGICAL

SUNDANCE FILM FESTIVAL

```
L H H A R D B E C D H V R K K T C L T H
N A N L M C X Q M X M Q N M C D W G U O
R D C L E L E E P N A D R O J T E W B R
Y A Q I Z Z U B X C A X Y A J T R M E R
P N F S G H W H E X K R L G O Z U I D O
A I F O E O W Z Q S O T L U L O T C L R
R E T N A I L I S T T A T K K N C H A F
E L X W P Q R O S X N A Q Z F J I A I I
H K X I J V A I H I C I C K Y H P E R L
T A F L T L H S G C O E E T F B T L O M
O L C L O K L I Q T Y K I A O U S A T D
N U S I R Q R E L M H S X U C R E B C B
P U J A Q O W R E V W L P N B T B E E Y
Y Y D M T E U H B M U I I N O R G L R C
H A U S T E R C E S Y L I M A F B S I T
Z M E L A K E I T H S T A N F I E L D K
X B S S E C C U S L A I C R E M M O C S
U A A C A D E M Y A W A R D S O U H P B
V C R I T I C A L L Y A C C L A I M E D
L A V I T S E F M L I F E C N A D N U S
```

Answers on page 189.

ONE CUT OF THE DEAD

One Cut of the Dead is a 2017 Japanese zombie comedy film written and directed by Shin'ichir Ueda. Made with an extremely low budget of only ¥3 million ($25,000) with a cast of unknown actors, the film opened to little fanfare until it received wider attention after being shown at the Udine Film Festival. Upon its re-release in Japan, it grossed over ¥3.12 billion ($27,935,711) in Japan and $30.5 million worldwide. It has the distinction of being the first film to earn over a thousand times its budget. The film follows a team of actors and filmmakers who are tasked with shooting a zombie film for live television in a single take.

ABANDONED (Plant)

CHINATSU

DECAPITATION

FAUX-REALITY

HIGURASHI

HORROR

JAPANESE

KO

LIVE SHOW

LIVE TELEVISION

NAO

PENTAGRAM

SINGLE-TAKE

TRUE FEAR

ZOMBIE CHANNEL

ZOMBIE COMEDY

ZOMBIE CREW

```
Z K N Q X F X N N G C F M O B K
T R P K V T Q O P X J D I K L C
T Y T P Q J H I J A P A N E S E
F Z Y B I V I T V B L L N T L D
L F A U X R E A L I T Y F E R E
X S I N G L E T A K E U N T M N
W Y H M Q O D I A B P N G D A O
E H S H R H O P V F A L X F R D
R L A O Q A P A H H Z E D F G N
C I R R N A J C C I T Y O C A A
E V U R T R U E F E A R E G T B
I E G O O H I D O R T E R I N A
B S I R U B D V I U R N U K E R
M H H Y M W U S T A N I H C P P
O O N O I S I V E L E T E V I L
Z W Z O M B I E C O M E D Y W W
```

HEREDITARY

Hereditary is a 2018 psychological horror film written and directed by Ari Aster. The film was Aster's directorial debut and received wide-spread critical acclaim for several aspects of the film's production and performances. The film follows the Grahmans, who lose their youngest child in a car accident when their oldest son drives the car into a telephone pole. The family grieves and tries to heal. Annie Graham, the mother, conducts a seance to reconcile with her dead child only to invite darker, older forces into their household.

ANAPHYLACTIC SHOCK

ARI ASTER (writer and director)

CAR CRASH

COVEN

CRITICAL ACCLAIM

DECAPITATION

DIRECTORIAL DEBUT

EVIL DEMONS

FAMILY TIES

GRIEVING FAMILY

HEREDITARY

KING PAIMON

OCCULT RITUALS

OCCULT SIGILS

POSSESSION

PSYCHOLOGICALLY (Distressing)

SPIRITUAL ADVISER

TELEPHONE POLE

THE GRAHAMS

TONI COLLETTE (actress)

TRAGIC ACCIDENT

S G M Y O Q M M W Y M G V F Y T S P X N
T K J N S E I T Y L I M A F Q J F S N O
U S P I R I T U A L A D V I S E R Y O I
B M T R S V D F K P L H V F K S F C M S
E P J F V O W E Y V C J C D X W G H I S
D B S G O T H G T J C B C J C O R O A E
L G L Z Z O S K B G A K V E L J A L P S
A D A W A E T T E L L O C I N O T O G S
I S U T H E G R A H A M S E W V C G N O
R N T U F R D R D R C Q T W S F A I I P
O O I A G D E C A P I T A T I O N C K R
T M R K C O H S C I T C A L Y H P A N A
C E T K E C P U I D I A O S R L Z L H R
E D L S A L S E M V R R M V D Y I L C I
R L U T R A G I C A C C I D E N T Y T A
I I C H E R E D I T A R Y Q D N N Y J S
D V C O D G J K X R H A H H S N A O B T
M E O V A O C C U L T S I G I L S N E E
O X U D E L O P E N O H P E L E T A A R
Y L I M A F G N I V E I R G F Z W Y A W

Answers on page 190.

A QUIET PLACE

A Quiet Place is a 2018 American post-apocalyptic science-fiction horror film directed by John Krasinski and co-written with Scott Beck and Bryan Woods. Beck and Woods based the story on the silent films they enjoyed watching in college, and they used their experience growing up in rural Iowa as the film's setting. The film stars John Krasinski and Emily Blunt as Lee and Evelyn Abbott, who struggle to raise their kids and survive in a world that's inhabited by blind extraterrestrial creatures with a strong sense of hearing.

BEAU

BLIND ALIENS

COCHLEAR IMPLANT

DISTRACTION

EMILY BLUNT (actress)

EVELYN

FIREWORKS

JOHN KRASINSKI
(director, co-writer, & actor)

LEE

MARCUS

(Make) NO SOUND

POST-APOCALYPTIC

REGAN

SCI-FI HORROR

(American) SIGN LANGUAGE

SILENT BIRTH

TOY SPACE SHIP

```
G M Q M U V K C E V E L Y N Z T
O S S N E I L A D N I L B P N S
S R I Z U Q N W N A G E R A M P
K E K L Q Q C D B E A U L G I S
E M S F E U S Y A J P P A H L K
G I N D Z N K P K M U S H R R
A L I N Z K T L L I B E G V K O
U Y S U U I S B R F C F K E M W
G B A O E F W A I A L B I Y A E
N L R S C L E W P R L Q Y L R R
A U K O D L S S S N T P F E C I
L N N H M Y M Z Z A H T E U F
N T H C W O O V V L F M W C S E
G P O S T A P O C A L Y P T I C
I C J X X R O R R O H I F I C S
S N O I T C A R T S I D I H K K
```

US

Us is a 2019 psychological horror film written and directed by Jordan Peele. The film follows Adelaide Wilson and her family as they encounter a malicious group of doppelgangers. Adelaide was once so worried that something bad was going to happen, but little did she know from where that trouble would stem.

ADELAIDE WILSON

ANIMALISTIC

DOPPELGANGERS

ELISABETH MOSS (actress)

HORROR FILM

HOUSE OF MIRRORS

JORDAN PEELE (writer and director)

LUPITA NYONG'O (actor)

MENACING

PSYCHOLOGICAL

PYROMANIAC

SADISTIC

SOUTH BY SOUTHWEST (premiere)

TERRIFYING

THE TETHERED

TIM HEIDECKER (actor)

US

WILSON FAMILY

WINSTON DUKE (actor)

```
E K B H U V W N V Z I E F U F E V Q W U
P E E B O S L J A I V S I Q T Z T Y I T
Q L Y F G H O R R O R F I L M S W U B P
U W K H N G C X C E S A F R E J C W P H
H C L K O O U P R S M F Y W R J R N Y O
P I L Z Y O T O T C Z T H J Z E O P R U
B T X K N Q O Z P I H T E Y L S M J O S
C S Y H A U A K O D U L L I L E G R M E
T I A M T K J I E O E I S I N G N M A O
I L P U I J L X S E M A W A L F I L N F
M A P H P X Y Y P A B E C M G D Y C I M
H M A J U O B N F E D I Y Q U Q F V A I
E I A Z L H A N T I N I B Q T O I C C R
I N B X T D O H A G M T S R L I R Y X R
D A D U R S M L T H E T E T H E R E D O
E D O O L O E Z I E S G K U I C E N E R
C S J I S D W F C Z Y J P Q D C T Y E S
K A W S A B N V B E K U D N O T S N I W
E Q F S R E G N A L G E P P O D C W S X
R Z E P S Y C H O L O G I C A L K A W A
```

Answers on page 190.

MIDSOMMAR

Midsommar is a 2019 folk horror film written and directed by Ari Aster. The final cut of the film focuses on a deteriorating relationship inspired by a difficult breakup experienced by Aster. The film stars Florence Pugh and Jack Reynor as Dani and Christian, American college students and dysfunctional couple. They travel to rural Sweden with a group of friends to experience a once-in-a-lifetime midsummer festival. However, they instead find themselves in the clutches of a murderous and sinister cult.

ATTESTUPA

CHRISTIAN

COMMUNE

CULT

DANI

FOLK HORROR

HALLUCINOGENIC

HALSINGLAND

JOSH

MARK

MAY QUEEN

MIDSUMMER

MURDER

(Psychedelic) MUSHROOMS

PAGANISM

PELLE

SACRIFICES

SWEDEN

```
Z A L P D M U R D E R D D Y J S
R U N E K G D A F L H B F H F D
H A L L U C I N O G E N I C R N
A K U L E W P H L N P Z I T N E
L N V E I P U S K U A O N V L D
S I N A D S K O H A G R E P K E
I A V U M G H J O P A G E G N W
N M C E C U L T R U N Y U R A S
G F J R U T H X R T I D Q G I O
L S A J I I M U O S S F Y Q T F
A B H U O F R V R E M N A A S B
N U Q I E G I V C T Z J M C I C
D P V L O Q E C B T A M M U R J
E N U M M O C L E A C T A Q H X
I M U S H R O O M S Y P R F C R
V U R E M M U S D I M E K I X S
```

Answers on page 190

LITTLE MONSTERS

Little Monsters is a 2019 post-apocalyptic musical action comedy horror film written and directed by Abe Forsythe. The film premiered at the Sundance Film Festival in January 2019, and was released in a limited theatrical capacity in October 2019, followed by digital streaming a few days later. The film stars Lupita Nyong'o as Audrey Caroline, a kindergarten teacher who has to team up with a washed-up musician (Alexander England) to protect the students from a zombie apocalypse.

ACTION

AUDREY

BETRAYAL

COMEDY HORROR

DAVE

FARM

FELIX

FIELD TRIP

MILITARY

MUSICAL

MUSICIAN

TEACHER

TEDDY

TESS

U.S. TESTING (Facility)

ZOMBIES

```
K R D C P Y E Q Q Y U C I R H R
W O C P R V A C T I O N L W L A
O R H K A U W K Q Z H U N Q Y M
Y R T D B S I Z O P U O J S V Z
M O E C L T V J R E H C A E T F
B H D F T E N A I C I S U M N I
U Y D A P S O A Z R E M E F V U
B D Y R M T T E S S Z T Y B X S
X E D M F I E L D T R I P U R E
E M T Q X N L K X H F U P H H I
K O R R G G E I I X U B V A A B
O C W N A K F F T G E N A U Y M
W F U M P Y H V E A B Z C D J O
U E H Y V M A Z G L R Y E R V Z
C L N K H Z J L I U I Y D E C X
X C R L A C I S U M H X R Y N V
```

Answers on page 191.

THE LIGHTHOUSE

The Lighthouse is a 2019 film directed and produced by Robert Eggers. Beginning as a reimagining of Edgar Allan Poe's unfinished short story, "The Lighthouse," it evolved to be based on a nineteenth-century myth of an incident at Smalls Lighthouse in Wales. The film stars William Dafoe and Robert Pattinson as nineteenth-century lighthouse keepers in turmoil after a storm strands them at a remote New England outpost.

ALCOHOLISM

HALLUCINATE

HORROR

INSANE

LIGHTHOUSE

MERMAID

MURDER

NEW ENGLAND

PSYCHOLOGICAL

SCRIMSHAW

SURVIVAL

THRILLER

WAKE

WICKIE

WINSLOW

```
R Z U D O B C E X W F L E M E G
T I J N U V P S K K I H M N B A
L H S A H S A U I R E N A H G B
M A C L O E W O P K R S S F Z V
E F R G R I G H S M N Q J L W L
R C I N R P F T Y I K S J M O X
Z O M E O G Q H C V E U Q U Q W
S Y S W R L R G H G O R I R H P
P T H E S U L I O C S V W D Z M
E T A N I C U L L A H I I E O N
K E W E K A W W O R X V C R T H
K D M T E T J X G O W A K A M I
H Q R Z E Z H T I L F L I H F B
R E L L I R H T C Q Y C E N W F
D I A M R E M Y A L C Y I S T S
T A A L C O H O L I S M E R Y J
```

Answers on page 191

HIS HOUSE

His House is a 2020 horror thriller film written and directed by Remi Weekes from a story by Felicity Evans and Toby Venables. It premiered at the Sundance Film Festival in January 2020 before being released on Netflix in October 2020. It stars Wunmi Mosaku, Sope Dirisu, and Matt Smith, and it tells the story of a refugee couple from South Sudan struggling to adjust to their new life in England with evil lurking just beneath the surface.

APETH

ASSIMILATION

BOL

CULTURE-SHOCK

ENGLISH CHANNEL

GHOSTS

HAUNTING

LONDON

MASSACRE

RACISM

REFUGEES

RIAL

SOUTH SUDAN

SUSPENSE

THIEF

TORMENT

VISIONS

```
N S L I C L L B E F N I P X N J
O T Y U A E T H I E F J K S A N
S S E T M N X F J D B P N V D O
E O D I S N E T D G A O E L U M
S H I R I A D Y K W I P L S S L
N G Z I C H M A S S A C R E H S
E P C A A C Q J I G F V D F T Y
P Y Y L R H F V N B G P U B U W
S I R Q A S S I M I L A T I O N
U G E K E I G N I T N U A H S I
S S F C U L T U R E S H O C K R
C V U B X G K O M T P J A T E U
T F G C D N T N E M R O T B E J
K L E G F E E S F H T E P A L E
Y D E T W D S Z U X L O N D O N
I B S U Q R T B B W V J R P R H
```

THE INVISIBLE MAN

The Invisible Man is a 2020 science-fiction horror film written and directed by Leigh Whannell. It's based on the H. G. Wells' novel of the same name, a reboot of the 1933 film of the same name, and the eighth installment in *The Invisible Man* franchise. It stars Elisabeth Moss as Cecilia Kass, a woman who is stalked by her former partner, Adrian Griffin, who has acquired the means to turn invisible.

ADRIAN	INVISIBLE
CECILIA	JAMES
COBALT	OPTICS ENGINEER
DRUGGED	SLIT THROAT
ESCAPE	STALKED
FAKED DEATH	SUIT
FRAMED MURDER	TOM
GASLIGHTING	TRAPPED

```
J E R X I D A G B C E V Z U F W
H S E M A J Y N X S E T N J Z U
D A P W P O P I M I S C V E U G
D R U G G E D T G D T I I U W R
E H H L Q E T F V G N L L R I
F M K R P L K G R J Y V C F I P
B O L P A S W I A H P I L A N A
J T A B H L R L M I O S Z K G G
P R O P T I C S E N G I N E E R
T C E A Q T J A D Y C B S D N V
W W S Y E T T G M I Z L T D A U
Y B C U S H S K U S P E A E I Y
T P A U W R U N R M P Z L A R T
S E P V Y O I G D X B E K T D Y
K S E B U A T Y E Y V M E H A Z
F I Y Z G T F C R L H U D B T W
```

Answers on page 191

PREY

Prey is a 2022 American science-fiction action film in the *Predator* franchise. It's a prequel to the first four films and the fifth film in the mainline series. Directed by Dan Trachtenberg and written by Patrick Aison, it stars Amber Midthunder, Dakota Beavers, Dane DiLiegro, Michelle Thrush, Stormee Kipp, Julian Black Antelope, and Bennett Taylor. The story revolves around a young Comanche woman, Naru, who has to protect her people from a vicious, humanoid alien (Predator) and French fur traders.

BAIT

COMANCHE

DROPSHIP

FLINTLOCK PISTOL

FUR TRAPPERS

GREAT PLAINS

GREEN BLOOD

HEALER

HUNTER

LOWER BODY HEAT

MUPITSL

NARU

PAAKE

PREDATOR

SARII

TAABE

WAR CHIEF

```
M K U R N X V Z W S T Z X J F R
S T O Z A M B K M U P I T S L G
A U A L R P I H S P O R D I Z I
R M F Q U U P B R E L A E H Z S
I Z P R E D A T O R C Q M K N V
I L O T S I P K C O L T N I L F
W W Y Q F Y T O M T N D A F L U
A D W I Y D B V I V O L Y X K R
R X V G H A I A A O P I L Z G T
C T A A B E B Q L T C I X M P R
H R N Z M P C B A Q O B Q U J A
I E V M H Z N E P A A K E K Q P
E T L O W E R B O D Y H E A T P
F N I W E G Z U H Z R R D F E E
Y U X R N H C E H C N A M O C R
W H G B X T M E V A Z V Z Z S
```

Answers on page 192.

TALK TO ME

Talk to Me is a 2022 Australian supernatural horror film directed by Danny and Michael Philippou, written by Philippou and Bill Hinzman, and based on a concept by Daley Pearson. The film stars Sophie Wilde, Alexandra Jensen, Joe Bird, Otis Dhanji, Miranda Otto, and Zoe Terakes as a group of teenagers who discover they can contact spirits using a severed and embalmed hand.

ADELAIDE

CONNECTION

EMBALMED HAND

HAYLEY

I LET YOU IN

JADE

JOSS

MIA

MUTILATE

MYSTERY

NINETY SECONDS

OVERTAKEN

POSSESSION

RILEY

SPIRITS

STABBING

TALK TO ME

R A P F Z B R Q M P L T N O H L
C N O I T C E N N O C X M K K N
S H X Z L F E J S S S L E J J I
D P W U R O Y O C S X F E B A N
W S I M D N A H D E M L A B M E
V W M R X E E M U S Q R E R I T
T A M N I V Q E R S J A M M E Y
L X X T G T D H A I O A O B D S
R J A D E Z S C T O S I T J I E
F C Y R E T S Y M N S M K C A C
A Q J S T A B B I N G E L R L O
M U T I L A T E U D H C A U E N
K H E Z B H A Y L E Y K T T D D
O U E B A N I U O Y T E L I A S
Z Z O V E R T A K E N I E H O N
S D S A W Q A K H Z Y E L I R I

Answers on page 192.

M3GAN

M3GAN is a 2022 American science-fiction horror film directed by Gerard Johnstone and written by Akela Cooper. It originated from a story about a killer doll that Cooper and James Wan wrote while brainstorming story ideas. It stars Allison Williams and Violet McGraw as Gemma and Cady, and Amie Donald (physically) and Jenna Davis (voice) as M3GAN. It follows a young girl and her artificially intelligent doll who develop a strong bond. The doll, developing self-awareness, becomes hostile towards anyone who comes between her and the girl.

AI (artificial intelligence)

BRUCE

CADY

CAR CRASH

DEAD PARENTS

DEFENDS

EMOTIONAL (Attachment)

EVIL DOLL

FUNKI

GEMMA

HUMANOID ROBOT

MOTION CAPTURE (Robot)

MURDER-SUICIDE

ROBOTICIST

SCI-FI HORROR

SCREWDRIVER

SELF-AWARENESS

Answers on page 192.

RENFIELD

Renfield is a 2023 American action comedy horror film directed and produced by Chris McKay, and written by Ryan Ridley from a story by Robert Kirkman. It follows the character Renfield (played by Nicholas Hoult) who has been Count Dracula's (Nicolas Cage) immortal servant for over ninety years. He teams up with police officer Rebecca (Awkwafina) to fight off a violent crime family and sever ties with his vampiric master.

ACTION

BELLAFRANCESCA

CODEPENDENCY

COMEDY HORROR

CORRUPT POLICE

DRACULA

EATS BUGS

FAMILIAR

IMMORTALITY

MOBSTERS

REBECCA

RENFIELD

SERVANT

SUPER SPEED

SUPER STRENGTH

SUPPORT GROUP

TEDDY LOBO

VAMPIRES

```
T B E W R P O E R E B E C C A N
E D P D A Q N C B E O B H D V E
D L E Y I N O I T C A W T M M P
D E Z C L D T L Q L D B G V Y U
Y I E N I O K O K C W B N U D O
L F H E M S U P E R S P E E D R
O N R D A M S T V A V P R S S G
B E N N F V E P F L Z I T N G T
O R T E Y J R U H U H W S M U R
S D J P V Z V R J C C Q R O B O
A C S E C N A R F A L L E B S P
J J N D H F N O S R B Q P S T P
R W P O H Q T C Q D L L U T A U
N S X C S E R I P M A V S E E S
S R O R R O H Y D E M O C R H E
Y T I L A T R O M M I P Y S D T
```

ANSWERS

The Cabinet of Dr. Caligari (page 4)

```
Z X P V Y Z T P C E R A S E C T
Z C T J J G S T F A Q R D R E D
M M M I Q N I S E Y L E I K A T
F L I F G W I N I S K K I C S N J
H I R N Y B O L J X Z A G E M A
G F I I G B I U I N J Z L A F N
H T W D N A S B U T I I D X R E
Y L N N U T S M I O S B B W N I
P U F E N S E A H S V M A N G O
N C R A T W E R N E R K R A U S S
O T A S V T P M H M U L Y S A C
T L N I S G X O K S P L V K J L
I D C W P V E S E S U O H T R A
S F I T X M G E R M A N I Q U S
T T S J T D I E V D A R N O C B
E N E I W T R E B O R H L K T L
```

Freaks (page 8)

```
K O Z N G K T C P N V W T Q D T
U Z U R O R R O H Y D O B M Q B
M W A M A R D N O J A H J O G J
U C T G P W Z J S Z Q S E N F W
M I S N G A R O E H X E D S O C
X E S M I F L P I L A A D O T R K
E S A N J L R N U B Z I C E P B
K A Y W V A H E C D O S E R J P
D L H O J C O D R U S L R G W S
W A C A R K E R T E F P A P G N J
A R L B N F R W H Y R V H A N G
R U I D E O O I Y O P I H D D U
F U E O I R R N N O L N E S A F
I C L T W D M S B Y V R M D Z T
I T S I T R A E Z E P A R T A F
T J L A R T A P O E L C H V A O
```

Frankenstein (page 6)

```
G M I L N V M H M A Y H Z L D U
R A X O K C W U Z R E S F P U R
A E A T C M Q L O Y T F R I T Z
V C C L F B T R R O E Z G C F
E L Y U X S A N A L D I F I C S
R A V C N R E P R O M J Q R E O
O R U G O H E A C W A G M E L H
B K X B X S K E B M R E U W A U
B E A O P S R H O A Y C R O H N
E L H R I P B G M T S M D T W C H
R R O R C O I M C K H D E H S H B
L C O L I N C L I V E N R C E B A
D B A V A R I A N A L P S T M A C
L L I M D N I W O S L G C A W L
M O N S T E R A C U E C A W O W I
X S V D K N E U I W Y E M O W I
```

The Mummy (page 10)

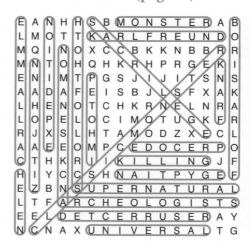

```
E A N H H S B M O N S T E R A B
L M O T T K A R L F R E U N D O
M Q I N O X C C B K K N B B R R
M E N T O H Q H K R H P R G E K I
E A N I M T P G S J I J I T S N S
A A D A F E I S B J L S F X A A K
L H E N O T C H K R N E L N R A
L O P E L O C I M O T U G K L O
R A J X A E L H T A M O D Z X E C L
C T H K R U I K I L L I N G J F
E Z C C S H N A I T P Y G E
H E L Z B N S U P E R N A T U R A L
L T F A R C H E O L O G I S T S
E E L D E T C E R R U S E R A Y
N C N A X U N I V E R S A L T G
```

172

ANSWERS

KING KONG (page 12)

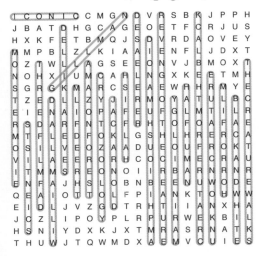

```
B E E A C A G X W Z D D P U E U
L E H B S O N O F K O N G R M E
S K U L L I S L A N D I C O P L
B R J V T C J U N T A U E R I G
Y I A N N D A R R O W S Z R R N
T A P D R K G R Q X E Y E O E U
I L E L V P O D L K C C W H S J
C N F D A E V N A D I L A F T T
K I A E X G N N M G S E Q Z A A Q
R A D R X S E T S X I N C M T K
O T O Y E R F A U O J L H N E I
Y N C Z F I L R Z R J Z G A X D
W U E I Q C T N T H E Z O Q M N
E O R R R E T S N O M C K M I Z A
N M P Q S R U A S O N I D Q X P
L L O C S I R D K C A J W Z A K
```

LES DIABOLIQUES (page 16)

```
L S P Y H D D A L E H C I M Z L
D M S S X O Y R E T S Y M Z V O
E D D E Y F R Z M O R B I D B X
S N R I D C A R W Q H C N E R F
A D W O G A H R O S Z X R Y Z O
E V V U W L T O L R C K Z U H W
L U A U P N D E L A S S A L L E
E R I P S N O C S O L A G A M V
R S E T U P C P Y G G M Z Z D K
E S P R O C G N I S S M H X D
R S X W H O D U N I T H C E O Q
D P T I F W W G N I T N U A H D
L X T L P R E D R U M O A L L N
E W P R E L L I R H T H S G A S
M A N I T S I R H C E L O C I N
N R H K W P Q A C V K Q U Q D N
```

CREATURE FROM THE BLACK LAGOON (page 14)

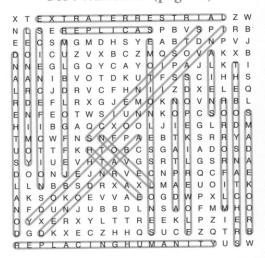

```
I C O N I C C M G N D V R S B K J P P H
J B A T D H G C A G E O E T F C R J U S
H X K F E T B M Q J S D V R D A O V E Y
M M P B L Z L K I A A I E N F L J D X T
O Z T W L L A G S E E O N V J B M O X T
N O H X I U M C A H L N G X K E E T M H
S G Z G K M A R C S E A E W R H R M Y E
T Z I E N A I O P A F E U F G L M T I L B
E I S D A R F N T C F B H T O F O A F A E
M T F L E D F O K L G S H L H R E R C A T
O S I L L V E O Z A A D U E O U F R O K T
V I L A E M S R E O N O C O C I M E C R A U
I E N F A J H S L O B N B E E N U W O D E
Q E A I O T T O L F P I A N K T O H W W
J C Z L I P O Y P L R P U R W E K B I L
H S N I Y D X K J X T M R A S R N A T K
T H U W J T Q W M D X A E M V C U I E S
```

INVASION OF THE BODY SNATCHERS (page 18)

```
X T E X T R A T E R R E S T R I A L Z W
N L S E R E P L I C A S P B V S P I R B
E E C S M G M D H S Y E A B T D N P V J
D O I C U Z V X B C Z M Q S O V A K X B
N N E G L G Q Y C A Y O I P A J L K I S
L R C J D R V C F H N I I Z D X E L E Q
R D E F L R X G J E M O K N O V N F B L
E N F E O T W S I U N K O P C S O O S
H I I B G A Q C X O O L J I E G L R D M
T M C W F N S N F P A E B T K S R R Y A
U O T T L H T A V G S D H A S R A D D L
S Y I O N U I J N R V E C N R P R Q C E
D O N L N B B D R X A X L M A E U O I T K
A K S O K O E V A E O G D W P X L C O
N F D U N J U B B D L N S A O F M M H O
O Y X E R X Y L T T R E E K L P Z I E R
D G D K X E C Z H H Q S U C F Z Q T R B
R E P L A C I N G H U M A N I T Y U S W
```

ANSWERS

The Blob (page 20)

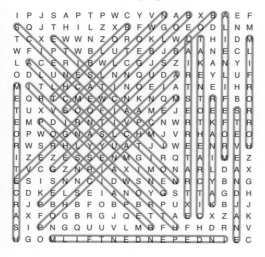

Psycho (page 24)

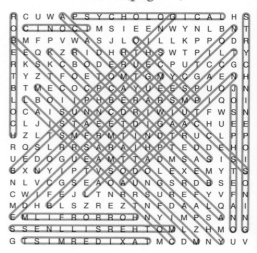

Eyes Without a Face (page 22)

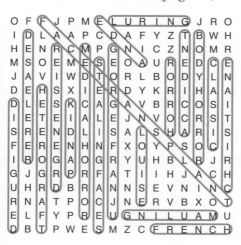

The Birds (page 26)

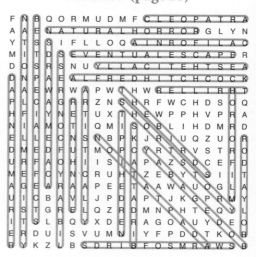

174

ANSWERS

KWAIDAN (page 28)

```
U S X J M P N L A N N O I K U Y
B E U K T R A P P E D Z I J Z O
R I L K I S S L A D N A S G X F T
I A A P G L R R Z J T T N C D J
L T S C Q H E X W I F E I U E P
R K O P K U O Q F Y Y W G P V M
H L M K G H T S Q S A N A O O K
H O R R O R A C T A M W D F M N
S F L E U D G I Q S U U I T E O
S T S O H G E E R H T P P E R K
Y S I J A P A N E S E O A A S I
X O C S N O B B I R D E R D R C
G J A N T H O L O G Y Q K I A H
T E A H O U S E N D N I L B E J
S F C Y D K H O I C H I H B I S
H Y D Y M R O T S W O N S U K Q
```

NIGHT OF THE LIVING DEAD (page 32)

```
I D T T D B B N G Y U F D J T U
M E R I F N O B F L O A N I N B
O E C X S L U O H G E C N L E W U
L C A P Q V K M F D N S H B D N J
O T E Z K E W T N P I R H O A R N O
O L T U E C I N O S O J X I P E Z
V O H Z Q K J X L S B P B N E O M
S I A F L E S H E A T E R S D N B
X V C A N N I B A L I S M C N G I
Y P W A J K A K R C M K A R I E
N W M N K U O V B T G Q N A G O S
T E S L D D M R L I J N L O L
H Y X Q J Y Y Y A U X E A L R L
O K B U Z K V H B C B R J E E C
J D O R E M O R B T A G Z C K W
```

ROSEMARY'S BABY (page 30)

```
A Y Y B A B C J V Z K Q U D C G
Y L V A T C P T E H W H E S R S
N P M G R D Q E D I C I U S B F
S U A E S U O H D O O W Y U G J
T E R R Y T S I R H C I T N A B
N T G Y Q Q F E N A O R T X S H
E G A K Z E B R A M F O R D L I
T A N V U T N A D N E P W V I M
A T A I S C Y R A M E S O R G
A E R R A E B K K W C F N A H N
E R A A N T T O O R S I N N A T
R H A N J H A U R A J O T M F J I
T U I Z J O F F U D K T Q N Q
O O T F K B S G C X G G J F H L W
X S B Z H G X Z W C O V E N H E
```

THE WICKER MAN (page 34)

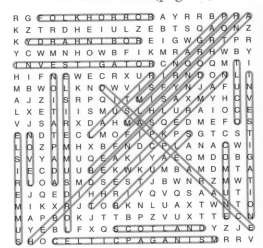

```
R G F O L K H O R R O R B A Y R R B P H A
K Z T R D H E I U L Z E B T S Q A O N Z
K Y D R A H N I B O R E I G W G R T P R Y
Y C W M N H O W B F I K M R A R H W B Y
I N V E S T I G A T O R C N O O Q M T I
H I F N E W E C R X U R I R N D O N U
M B W O L K N D W I S F Y N J A F N
A J Z I S R P Q T M I S A X M Y H C O C E
L X E T I I S M U S L H L U R A I O C E S
V J S A R X D A H M A S Q E D M E F O S
E N D T E C L M O F I P K P S G T C S T I
L O Z P M H X B E T C P L A N A C W B
S V J A M U Q E A K I Y A E Q M D O S A
I E C D U R E K W K U M B A M D M T G A
R L O A S M D S E S T J B W M Z M W T I
E J Q E D I H H R I Y Q V Q S A A U T I
M I K X R J M R O K N L U A X T W N T O
M A P B O K J T T B P Z V U X T T E C N
U Y E B U F X Q S C O T L A N D Y Z J E
S H O C E L T I C P A G A N I S M R R V
```

ANSWERS

THE EXORCIST (page 36)

```
I X P P D N A G E R F N Y P G T
V Z A D W X C D X B I N K W D
I P W B N X H H E T K R I L N M
O M U L O I V R N I A R T U C R
L T H A M F R I N E R E R T H F
E M B R E I Z S I I R M O I C A
N M U D C P F N H A R G M U T T
T F F T N U B T G M S E L O L H
R O M A N R I T U A L H Y V T E
B Q C N I C C O C N N T C D C R
U S D R A W K C A B D A E H L D
E E N E I Z Y Q Y M L F R X A Y
H L W P A A T S E I R P I F S E
N B D U H G M I G O G S N A S R
L P A S L N O I L L A D E M I R
U E F L E X O R C I S M R G C A
```

JAWS (page 40)

```
M T V P W V K D T T N H B K N G
R E P O O H H N H V Y L O I I E
Z V I L F B A A R A T S L R L C
B B P Q V R R L I U N I B L C S
Q T G U K P P S L G U L C E J J
X C E I F H O I L H O G N R K I
G A X N U M O Y E N B A A M L N
R G P T J A N T R L C K R V Q D
E E L T C A N I M A T R O N I C
A V O K N F P M S K L T K Z H K
T Z S O A B E A C H K N J P Y H
W S I J E O T I G E R S H A R K
H A O A C A X U C L W D F S A J
I T A N B O T O B R O D Y Z H M B
T F K Q P G S P I E L B E R G M
E R E H P A R G O N A E C O O D
```

THE TEXAS CHAINSAW MASSACRE (page 38)

```
D Y L A X K G E T C F K A T V H
F L C L P P S S J Y M U I V R O
W L B M D R X U E F V R S R Z R
S A K S A N U O R Q P E U R K Q
H O L F K I H R Y E B S X K R
O F O A X W R R Y C P B O T O X
R R H T B P O W E R T O O L S V S
R A E A C O N T L Z R F F M O
O N L A L X D H V B Y E J N M U
R K M A A B S G H X Y H A P T
A I X C S M D U P P J A P U V H
M N I H C S L E A T H E R F A C E R
J N I H I I U L G J Q G I F J R
Q M Z C C V U S S L A S H E R N
J X S W A S N I A H C F N N C L
Q N O V F I N A L G I R L N G T
```

THE OMEN (page 42)

```
S U P E R N A T U R A L B L V J
M C L T E D I C I T N A F N I R
T M L S C X Z H P W N H S S X T
R R G I S R H L J U O A F L E S
E O K R S U O B J Y N E A M N S
B T U H O C K R R V X G O M M A
R W O I T N U Z H A S D R B Y A C
M E F M O N Q A R J H O D N Y R T
V I D N Q A R J K A T H Y S T E
C L J A O N L C B T A F Y M L A
W E E M O R F H A Y N A R E O K
P R G B F I T S A N N Y V A C A
F L X F G A E P A A O C D C S Y
G Z O Y Z C Z N N F G I Z S Y I
H F A T H E R S P I L E T T O U
```

ANSWERS

CARRIE (page 44)

```
Q K T U P M J U G K V S U C V B
Y Z N X R D O O L B G I P O E P
L G I J O M A R G A R E T Z F I
L N S E M F X B B B B F S N M E
I I X T E I R R A C M N O S I L
B K J U P U C Q C H R I S S U E
Z N V C C F R I U T T D L Y R K
T E S O L C R E Y A R P M O M I
A H B R B F X G U C W M R L N N
R P A T S Y I R B L O R C G K E
V E V C U P T R O T O T G D C S
Q T H E Z S C K E H R D S F X I
V S T L N K B U L L Y I N G F S
S U P E R N A T U R A L T J W C
G P M V I W J D B M V B T S Q U
E S U B A Z I H R E M P Y Q O S
```

THE HILLS HAVE EYES (1977) (page 48)

```
G L B H Q R K V Y K H S D I T U
R M H O R R O R G X S Z H O U P
C V E A L D S U N R E U V L R L
H T K D V U O C E R U B Y B M U
W X N N V D M T D A E T M Q F T
Z H I E L F R W P Y Z J M U U O
J X T R J A P M A S S A U L T T
B J Q B C P M C P M L J I X K X
G O A Z Z L E N A K A M Y X C T
B F B Z X E R E J M B R Z K A R
T F O B M H C O U A I N B N X E
M A B Y Y T U O F A I A N A I M S
A D K C D E R F I A N A I M P E
V E S U B A Y D T G A B N R C D
J B B U P X Q W E S C R A V E N
Z O L Y N N E B R U B O P H O G
```

SUSPIRIA (page 46)

```
G B I Q Z S R C F L N W F D Q T
P X N M U K D P R C H Y R E J C
A P O B L E H I R S D E O F G S
P Y I K G I G O F U H Q N I I U
Q T T N P L R B N P T D N I Z Z
T T A W A R N H E E G J S Z M Y
W H M N O C H H K R T M W E P A
O L I H S O S U I N E O C A L I
D F N L T N D B T A L C C L E Z
A M A P A S O M A T I L R C E D
H L E M B P Y C A U A E U J J T
S O R X B I C G I R B T L J M A
N E A H E R N G A A A N T D N N
G J V Z D A O N L W I T C H N E
X S W W C C L T H G I L Y K S R
A Q V H B Y B S R J T T X H I R
```

DAWN OF THE DEAD (page 50)

```
U M M O N O A Q S E I B M O Z O
R R A I J M A P O C A L Y P S E
I B L M E S C A P E S E L H G E
P J L G N A G R E K I B T E T H
K E H N T H Q P M R V J Z L M E
U R P L R C D H W A O U X I Z B
W E G J I D U I M O M E J C B R
N A T I O N A L G U A R D O S E
R N R G U S G A T S M Y P P T M
E I O N T U N D R C R U V T E A
T M G A U R Q E R O L L B E P K
E A E R G U A L E A M A G R H E
P T R F U I P P V G E S T E T Y
Q I T K O V K H W P K E R S N Y
Z O J Y U A B I R Y T I C O I K
M N V X Y L X A M D J A G O V C
```

ANSWERS

HALLOWEEN (page 52)

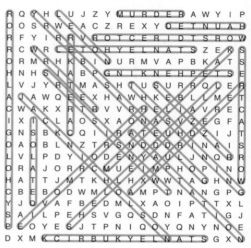

Grid puzzle answer for Halloween.

THE SHINING (page 56)

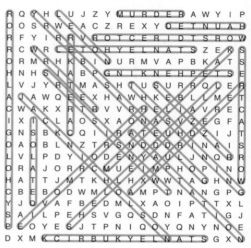

ALIEN (page 54)

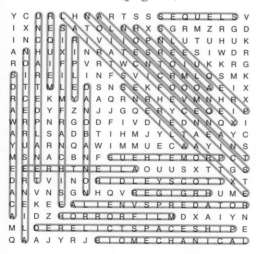

AN AMERICAN WEREWOLF IN LONDON (page 58)

ANSWERS

Poltergeist (page 60)

Videodrome (page 64)

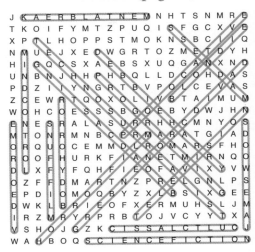

The Thing (page 62)

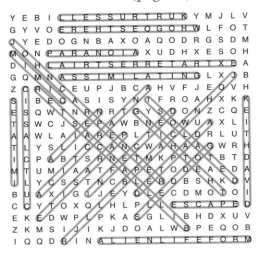

A Nightmare on Elm Street (page 66)

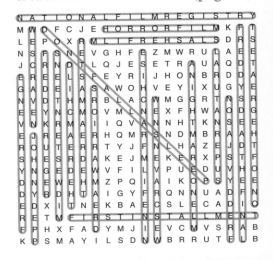

ANSWERS

The Fly (page 68)

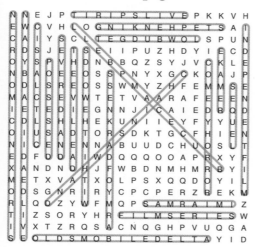

The Lost Boys (page 72)

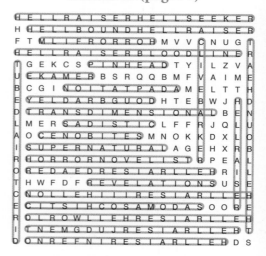

Evil Dead II (page 70)

Hellraiser (page 74)

ANSWERS

CHILD'S PLAY (page 76)

```
E J M T P E T M Z M A K B O U D
Q Q X Q O R R D E G N L D S D E
A F M H A M E Y W N D K F L J S
N E S E D C H U C K Y M X A F S
R V H W N R U O S G W M S R E S
E I G X C I A L L G Z G F H A S
R T Y P G M L W T L L Z S E N A
E C W L S I H L K C A E D R C O
D E V R F N G O F I L N L A H P
R T E V P A H O R M L A D D I C
U E M S L R V O K T L S C S O B
M D O O L J D R X D U V E S E B
E S R R V O O D O O G J Y R I U
C F R R N Y E D A V F U H S X C
L V I O O U L L L O D C Y H G P
W K S R S U P E R N A T U R A L
```

TREMORS (page 80)

```
H A J W K I K Z Q U F A F E L M
H S U R V I V A L I S T Y H L V
N E D L R A E R E H T A E H U B
T I J S W W N C T R E S E D V O
N M U V U K K S D X Y D H O S D
R O N U N D E R W O O D U I S X
P L D V L O R E T S N O M T E L
I O E A I E I H O R R O R C L Q
P E G R L F U G W E D Q X B E E V
B O I G P P R M X I K J R U F Y Y
O M R T B S S R D Z J Z G R R E E
M V U O H Y D E M O C Y A T E W S
B Z N Q R G R A B O I D R A N P D C
Z I D H Q C S S P Y C C F D N Z
```

PET SEMATARY (page 78)

```
W Z A L O U X U O I G R U I B E H B B Z
C S X T E P E H T N I D E I R U B W E A
I E N W X C H I C A G O D E O L E T Y M
Q I D C O L N O V E L S O X C S U R S D
J D A A D R D S U E U I A W U L A A V A
N U I M Y L T R P G K M O E T Q G K E B
S O U T Y E U D E U B H H P A K G I N D
A S Y V H R N R L A I O E R D P R D O H
I V T U V A E L E E N S H Y N C E R T T
A C O E T S I B H P T M E B L A R S A O
J F C U P N I T M E N T A N R M A T C R
P A R G O H D Q P A J E C S A C Q H R R
W A L I S N E I I B L S T I Y M A F F F
L H S D I H B N U N R Y N D P A K T I K
I B W H Y C H F K O S E R X A L U C L C
Q F E T R G L G L I U E Z A C B K A M A
D B H N V J V B A W N Y I X M O R P R B
L Z A H E O A E D N U G U L K D Q G O D
N F Z C G B F J S E N O I T A T P A D A
```

JACOB'S LADDER (page 82)

```
G C E T L A A U G I Y N Z G S W
Y W A H A D N O I S S E R G G A
H I Z G A I N F A N T R Y M A N
A S K C A B H S A L F C D A D Q
L S V Y B P Y W T F J L V T E T
L L J V Q S S C B I A T I J A S
U Y A E C J K Y G A C U S B D H
C H I R O P R A C T O R I P V Y
I P S Y C H I C Z H B Y O W H R
N J G D S T P J N Z H N L X E Z
A W D R K G Y C T N G O S X A D
T E S R A W Y G K D N Y R E Z I
I A D R I A N L Y N E M C R S A
O N R E F N I S E T N A D W O L
N D I H M S G V M A N T E I V R
S Z F T S F Q H L O U I S S Z P
```

ANSWERS

IT (page 84)

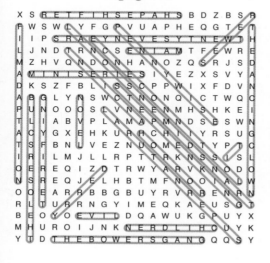

CANDYMAN (page 88)

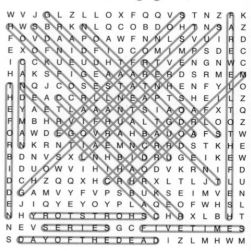

THE SILENCE OF THE LAMBS (page 86)

BRAM STOKER'S DRACULA (1992) (page 90)

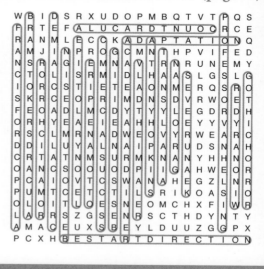

ANSWERS

THE NIGHTMARE BEFORE CHRISTMAS (page 92)

```
Z K K R R W B Z D B R M N Q I Y
E I G O O B E I G O O A I L S H
P J Y I O C E J G G R M E A I X
U A N S B C V I E U Y O T L H N
M C O A H O P P Z D P N S L T O
P K I L W E R T I W A S L O S I
K S T L E E N A K F D T E D T T
I L O Y H H Y R K S I E K G A H
N A M S W H L R Y R C R N A H M
K M P S T D A M A S N I R W I
N N T N Y S A N D Y C L A W S A
G T S G T S I G O L O C I X O T
H A L L O W E E N T O W N C H M
T I M B U R T O N Y L L A S K M
N O T G N I L L E K S K C A J Y
```

THE CRAFT (page 96)

```
K E N O N A M Q R V R F C E B K
K L B B W E A R T H D E I T Y S
S E R E D R U M J S K P K D P E
O M X A Y C N A N R E H E L S H
T E N G D M A T K M Q L T I B C
I N V O C A T I O N S P I R I T
A T F A E N E C S T H G I F N I
P S Y C H H O S P I T A L Z D W
K C R S J N G N I Y L L U B I
I H S A U L S L S L O J F N A
N R W B B X H S J T A T G D S A
A C S L L E P S V E J R I D S L
N L H A R A S S M E N T A Y P D
L E P R O C H E L L E S H H E S
I X B O N N I E C M N B D W L G
A Y H Y R G N U H R E W O P L I
```

SCREAM (page 94)

```
I T Z Q Y D H D G G Y D N A R E
T H Z V G G G M H E Y R N P E G
K O R O B S D O O W V C M X X J
N T A T U M D S S E H A N G E D
K S F O W A D D T S I S C Y P U
L R I G L A N I F C U R L L A T
Z B G V D R E A A R M B A L Q S
L Z L N O T R G C A O Q S I N G
F B S R W Y F A E V S Q S B O Q
A Q R L Y V C L D E I C I N T P
H O C Q A K O E W N D A C E T V
H D Y F V S U N K U N X D E O P
W E V H S G H S U Q E T Y R C K
Q W K E N N Y E L V Y D G U P X
W E S R M A N O R U A E F A C X
D Y T G S T A B B E D H J M C V
```

THE BLAIR WITCH PROJECT (page 98)

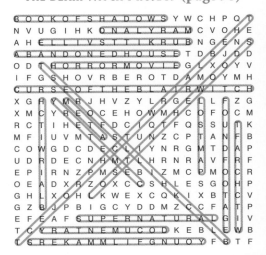

```
B O O K O F S H A D O W S Y W C H P Q T
N V U G I H K O N A L Y R A M C V O H E
A H E L L I V S T T I K R U B N G E N S
A B A N D O N E D H O U S E T B D B J D
O D T H O R R O R M O V I E G L X O Y V
I F G S H O V R B E R O T D A M O Y M H
C U R S E O F T H E B L A I R W I T C H
X G R Y M R J H V Z Y L R G E L L F Z G
X M C Y R E O C E H O W M H C O F O C M
R C T I H L T F D C I Q T F Q S S A N F
M F I U V M A S T U N Z C P T A N F P D
C O W G D C E C L I Y N R G M T D A P P
U D R D E C N H M T L H R N R A V F R F
E P I R N Z P M S E B I Z M C P M O C R
O E A D X R Z O X C C S H L E S G O H P
G Z B J P B I G C Y D D M Z C C F A T Y
E F E A F S U P E R N A T U R A L G I T
T C Y R A T N E M U C O D K E B L E W B
T S R E K A M M L I F G N U O Y F B T F
```

ANSWERS

THE DEVIL'S BACKBONE (page 100)

```
T A S F I G T K M E J C F Z D B
G H O S T U Q C X C A Q F O A P
G S P A N I S H Y N C Y E W D E
O Z D E K L B T A E I J W X M N
T R J J L F L O C N R Z I S O
H Y E C E E C U H O T V A A A H
I J D P D R H S G N O J N U C W
C T R S G M U A P N N T M B F O
H N U F K O J N C I V I L W A R
O I M O X D Z T A F R N P M V P
R A P I I E Z U R O C Z X Y P H
R P H F M L Y H L E P T J A J A
O S E L X T G D O C T O R H A N
R H C U Y O M K S R I I Q Y B A
U U B T Z R F N M O C E U C Y G
F C L D F O P T C F B M O B K E
```

28 DAYS LATER (page 104)

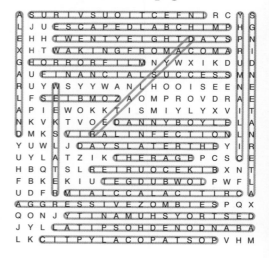

```
A S U R I V S U O I T C E F N  R C Y S
L J U E S C A P E D L A B C H I M P H G
E H H T W E N T Y E I G H T D A Y S H
X H T W A K I N G F R O M A C O M A R I
G H O R R O R F I L M N Y W X I K D U D
A U F I N A N C I A L S U C C E S S M R
R U Y S Y Y W A N L H O O I S E E N E
L S E I B M O Z A O M P R O V D R A E
A P I E W O K T I S M I Y L Y X I
N K V K T V O E D A N N Y B O Y L  A N
D M K S V I R A L I N F E C T I O N L N
Y U W L J D A Y S L A T E R T H B Y I R
U Y L A T Z I K T H E R A G E P C S C E
H B Q T S L R E I R U O C E K I B X N T
F B K E K I U T E G D U B W O P C S A
U D F B M I A L C C A L A C I T I R C A
A G G R E S S I V E Z O M B I E S P Q X
Q O N J Y T I N A M U H S Y O R T S E D
J Y L A T I P S O H D E N O D N A B A
L K C I T Y L A C O P A T S O P V H M
```

JEEPERS CREEPERS (page 102)

```
F Y J C S V I C T O R S A L V A T L K I
C O T E K C N Y S R R L N P W K L B V E
W N E G E S I R B L E S X Z G T O P W I
O K V L B P D V O U A M G E F R K S R K
S C P J X U E S Q B J S B V E H K A D B
E E Y Q X N S R G A E T H E R Q G Q C E
R R K V Q Z E E S I L R P E R E B O O T
A B H H V T G P Q C N E S C R N Y W Q R
A N E T N T N E G U R A U R P F Y M X P
L A A I R H O E U N E E P G P J N X Y
K H F B O P B R R N O L E H R P S Y M B
L A A O D Y L S Y P O Y N C E L U E R B
L N N I T V V R Y Y X Z G J B R L O R U
E O C D R E E A G M E V J T H S I N C
B H L I V N P W F Y O I L J S D T P W
P E I C P S C E T I U S R U P Z U F W S
E R S X W P D E M O N I C U L W B J J
Q E E M N R R J I W F S Z U B D B A G J
E E R H T S R E P E E R C S R E P E E J
```

THE RING (page 106)

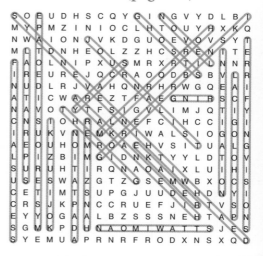

```
S O E U D H S C Q Y G I N G V Y D L B J
M Y P M Z I N I O C L H T O U Y H X K Q
N W A I O N J V K D G U O E V O V S Y T
M L T D N H E O L Z Z H C S R E N I T E
F A O L N I P X U S M R X R T I L N R
I R E U R E J Q C R A O O D B S B V L I
N U D L R J V A H Q N R H R W G Q E A I
A T I C W A R E Z T F A E G N I R S C F
N A V O T Y T F S I G V L I M J Q T I Y
C N S I O H R A L N E F C I H C C I G I
A E O U H O M N K R I W A L S I O G O N
L P I Z B I M G I D N K T Y Y L D T O V
S U R U H T I R Q N A O A I X L U I H I
U S E S W A Z G T Z G S E M W B X O C S
C E T I M I S U P G J U U D E H D N Y I
R S J K P D H N A O M I W A T T S J E S
S Y E M U A P R N R F R O D X N S X Q D
```

ANSWERS

SHAUN OF THE DEAD (page 108)

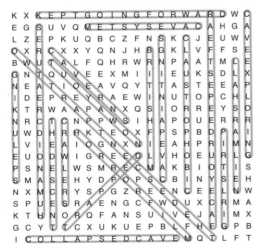

SLITHER (page 112)

THE DESCENT (page 110)

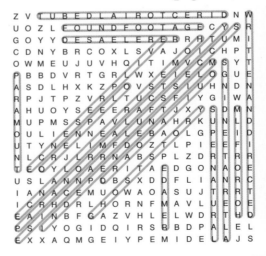

PARANORMAL ACTIVITY (page 114)

ANSWERS

Let the Right One In (page 116)

```
L R S S N Q Z A V Z N R E L E B Y Y T N
M T L D S P I H S N O I T A L E R C V V
L R E P R H V M O M M L I F R O R R O H
O I P I K A T D A W S N I B T U M D A D
H B D J H V T W N N L Q J Q E L I E S N L
K E O S D J T A X O U G B S A M I P I M
O A N N C E S E B G M E G D T W I P R I E
T F L E U D V X V L G C G G L T U T O M
S I I I J N Z E Y O A A U N T B Q H T U
N L N R Z R E X R L N C B T A J Q F H A
A M D E E W E X A A U H K D Y R O N G D
B F Q T I B R C P Y L T X E L G T N I A
R E V B O Z I K I L N A Z E B U Q S R P
U S I Q S T P L S U A E W N L E G R E T
B T S Q J M H D O C I D A T A R Q H A
U I T R D I A J H I S B N E R D U G T T
S V C G A I V P M R X Y Z E W D T G T I
S A T U R N A W A R D G G M D S S R E O
P U V N O S D E R F L A S A M O T I U N
```

Drag Me to Hell (page 120)

```
K B A E M Y D Q D J S G N I T N U A H F
D M E G V L C Q H P O S S E S S I O N J
T R O F Z E A V J I Q N Q F N L U R S L
X C A R B V L M C A B U T O Q M U O N I
Z U U G T M E D I L B G I X Q J S X O A K
R W J R M H O E E A J S A Q B C N N I K
Y R R M S E R Z A R I B O U G B O B T X
W I U S D E T E V V L G R D F R E S A U
K K S B T C D O E P U Y G D F R E S I M
G X D S A J Q L H D F E W R R E D G I M
D L L A K B B X C E A J K O O F E C C I
G K E X B I E R Y O L Y R U M A P E U A I
P Y U R H W E W W K L S Z D A Y M L I I
S P I R I T U A L A D V I S E R N D L I
M L O A N F O R G I V E N E S S S J A I
C H R I S T I N E B R O W N X N Y U H I
Y R P J L Y K V F O L K L O R E I H S D
O P U W I T X U D M S I T A R O P O R C
I L L A R U T A N R E P U S B I S P L C
Z Q W L V V G Q S A E N Z G X B D K E S
```

Thirst (page 118)

```
H N R C M A I D M U B I K D R R
R Z H E A L I N G B L O O D Y F
E T S E I R P C I L O H T A C K
D P A R K C H A N W O O K U E N
R T G E R I P M A V D F I Y E D
U N U Y H G N A S L T Q L T S R
M L N V G N W I R N R S B A A I
Z E S P R O C D E T A O L B E N
X H T W S C I H T E N O J U S K
I Y A E N I C C A V S Y Y R I S
O F I H I Z Y U Y N F I E N D B
G X N H V H J D L A U S B T L L
Z H E A L E R B Q E S I A V A O
P C Z C A T C Z Y R I O S U T O
F X P T Y E O G J O O N G P A D
C H O S P I T A L K N S G Z F K
```

Insidious (page 122)

```
T S Y Y O U N G G H O S T S K K
D L T H V B C F B B W P U T M T
S X I W Q L M B L F H U D I L S
U X T R P O R O R R O H F R I M
P N N E S O F X V L I F Y P J P
E T E H Y D A L T O N I P P O A
R R S T C Y E R V C Q G F S H R
N A D U R H H C N I H M Z R J A
A F O U I A N A O N X I A E N N
T O I F C N A W Z N Q A N C X O
U S R E E D E S O O X N C U L I
R T E H L P S E V M I E H T V D
A E L I R A M D E O R I R R M A
L R S E S I X A M D Z R S O M L
F A Y I E N Q J R F E D E T O W
R Z M A S T R A L P R O J E C T
```

ANSWERS

The Cabin in the Woods (page 124)

```
L D K R S H K D S I J Y Y N J M
I S K O U O R N I M C Y T W T A
E R F T R L O U T T U L R E C N
M E O C V D R O T W H R I A S D I
R T R E E E R R E H T M M P E C P
Q S C R I N O G R L H A S Y C U U
J N E I L W H R S A G F C L A L L
U O F D L H Y E O U K R I A P A A
L M I E A O D D N T K E F C I T I
E F E H N M E N A I Y N I O T I O
S E L T C H M U Y R Z K X P A O N
Z J D S E N O T N E I C N A T N
L O R T N O C F D V B U B T I K
R W E R E W O L F A Y B H C O R
I N C A N T A T I O N S K Z N G
Z O M B I E S Y E L D A H F W B
```

The Babadook (page 128)

```
B R W H B F H A T Y F C D C O R
H E C A I N M O S N I P I R S X
U T H A L L U C I N A T I O N S
M A N V B S N G K G W A C Z F R G
A N O G O X A R H R B J S V N R A
O I M Y T A L O N E D F I N G E R S
I Y R A M E L I A D W N P K K O S
D M A D A R K N E S S V V Z R H S
O N L E D J X E K W R B Y K E H A
N I I P O S S E S S I O N F C S N
S G B I A M P P E R U Z I E S I Y
T A D B S S E N D A M Q T N S R
E M E D E A D H U S B A N D N P S
R I D R L T O R M E N T O E C Q
        L E U M A S Z X J X X
```

The Conjuring (page 126)

```
M W I L R G V Y N H M L G Z W P
X F N D X T N X S O U A T J G O
S K U P E A B H T R R O H A S O
T U U Z M M M P C R I U H M E S
S I G G E N O Z A O C T V I N E
I R U S X L Y N F R B A I S I S
G H A K O K A U I H O N W W A S
O L C V N C P E T T C X R S A R D
L N A L F O I O I R S E I N R D
O I F I X S G A I D J O U I Z L
N L L F M A H P E W Q S F R P L
O M M T X R T S O D D B K I
M F Z D E C L A I R V O Y A N T T
E A V M U T B M U I D E M I U D
D L V O K V K F E C W A R R E N S
```

A Girl Walks Home Alone
At Night (page 130)

```
V M R J G N V M V O E P G A L S
Q C Y M N E R D M H A D I F H A
C N R K I M V A M P I R E R R E
K B P Q D D T M Y T U Q F O I E
T W T S R A V X T V B P R G Z D
A N S R A B T A R O L R R U T
C I B O O R R A T J O E E C H S
E E Y M B N J J A H O N D O E I
H T S L A E F H C N Y D A R K G N
B O I T A D E I I H U S M A I I
X H T I K T C Y H Q C R K A L E
F D Z C S D U I E S K E A S R F
R F I E A U L Q R T I P T H A S
R I W B S O V F O U N Z Y R C H
C C G R C H A D O R G W P B N T
```

ANSWERS

What We Do in the Shadows (page 132)

```
V H U V Z A W R O N M B U I T E O C K
A K N H W Y E A V O H S I G I I M C U
M C H V A E D R X G T O O T A U A K N
P I N L L M M W O I A L C L I A I U G
I R G Y Y S A O O G D T C N R A N M E
R E S M I N C L A D I A I L O W E E H
E H U T A D F R V L I V T P A C N N T
U N T R A Q L M R S U K L V E T I E A
N E N U V I R K V R R A W Y A M R R Y
T E R F R Q I H H D D E A C O N N D
E R U O A O A T P T F J G H X W T W
L R L R D R R S E R I P M A V G Z D
Z M E N S U P E R N A T U R A L
```

10 Cloverfield Lane (page 136)

```
E U A U F R J Y O A D V A T Y I
K S P M I U F G S A O A I D P O
C T O Y Y N W T P Z D U R A E F
A U C R E A T U R E S R O N T R U
T O A K J Y H C A T S H R R C R S
T K L X Y O M Q A E W D R R A C H S
A C Y L W E W M L S D O H C H I R
E A P W R S Z C R N R X H I T E O
I S R H A A E E A U N I F I E N H
I B E N H T F L W I U U F T I C A
S G K R N Q L O I T T Z Z I E N C I
S C K E R E H O T R Z C C N A C I
A Y T S H V C A O A C K S B C I A
M P T C Q Y D W T M A S Z E I T A G
S J I S E T A L I T U M Q R D C
T M K M P X P O W W D Q I G K E
```

The Witch (page 134)

```
T U E N G L I S H S E T T L E R S L T K
N N T R X W M Z P G I U L A H D V W U C
E B K C Z I S V I S Z V B V Z O D X B R
M A K T H T I K L G A Q U I X E Q K E I
P D I V C N F L E N U X T H U Q I D I T
L T R W R H A R I B Y D I S M Z T D L I
T I Y T E S T F H S A O I E L F S A O A
E E U E I O R O K O A W O M F L R P R L
S D T V U I U M C B Y I A E T C I O L F
D U V U I G P E A E L T C I O L F E T C
N A B R O L K S L R O C C H F R O E D O
L R A K C R C U T G T B T R H U E R R H
G B D V F A M A T G O R T N H D O B I I
N U K Z A O Y I H A A I A P Q T Y M V
E Y K L J Z I N V C L R Z T M N R V I Y
W J Y J I I T L V I J I E S A L C U G H F Q B I
E L P L L L T J I E S A L C U G H F Q B I
N B U Y Y U Y M N S Y Q W S N L B L P R
```

The Wailing (page 138)

```
E M A N O N J S N A K R S T W N
N X P C S E R G U N N E D M Q I
I N F C S V E N G O A C E P P N
R I M T E I M I N I H O H I G S L R
H X O A C L O L O S O N F O A N R O
S O O C S T U L M S N H A C I R R
H Q G G U P E I E E G O E B B L O
T A F O E A L L R I Y R E O N I O H N A
E F O E A I L R E O N I O H N A
D V J D C T L E Y P T L G G E A
R E A N I M A T E D C O R P S E
L F K N T B G S D K J P R D S R
R M N P I O E Y E U T I N Q E O
D Y K O R O D M R V H P W J S K
Q L I A C E X Y M S I C R O X E
```

ANSWERS

RAW (page 140)

```
H A N O E B P P V Y F R E N C H
C Z C X L I I Q E X J R J X I L
J U S T I N E T T I G B J D U T
H T F P E H D N E G F A P W T V
H O U A W K B U R U Q P X O V W
N S E T D C O M I N G O F A G E
A Z M A P A D V N W T D E C Q F
I Q I E O N Y Z A A M F L E S H
R K F M N N H H R Y W Y I O B C
A A B F E I O A Y F T A S R E J
T L N T I B R Z S Y K D B E X N
E E K I R A R I C Q P R J D T O
G X N B D L O N H A D A J R R E
E I Q M A I R G O O X M C U E P
A X H X S J K O P W A E M M V
Y Z J S F M T X L N P P G U E C
```

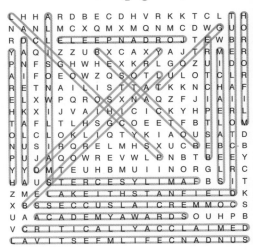

GET OUT (page 144)

```
L H H A R D B E C D H V R K K T C L T A
N A N L M C X Q M X M Q N M C D U O R
R D C L E L E E P N A D R O J T E W R
A Q E I Z Z M S X C A X Y A J T R M E R
P N F S G W H E X K R L G O Z U I D O
R E T N A I L I S T A T K K N C H A I
E L X W P Q R O S X N A Q Z F J I A L
H K X I J V A I H I C I C K Y H P E L
T A F L T L H S G C O E E F B T L O M
O L C L O K L I Q T Y K I A O U S A T D
N U S I R Q R E L M H S X U C R E B C
P U J A Q O W R E V W L P N B T B E E Y
Y D M T E U H B M U I I N O R G L R C T
H A U S T E R C E S Y L I M A F B S I T
Z M E L A K E I T H S T A N F I E L D S
X S S E C C U S L A I C R E M M O C S
U A A C A D E M Y A W A R D S O U H P B
V C R I T I C A L L Y A C C L A I M E D
L A V I T S E F M L I F E C N A D N U S
```

TRAIN TO BUSAN (page 142)

```
K E N G B L A J Z F T T S H D Q
R K O K N A D A Q G C J F O T A
E J D W B E T R A Y A L L T B G
Y H A A T R A P P E D H R D L R O
A C E N O N S M Y G E A P G F Z
L D R B I U W H D M F S C V Q
P E N H K A Q U A R A N T I N E
L U H O R X E I R Y N A S U B
A T R S T L R O Q X A E I F A
B K A L E K A V Y A W A W O T S
E T F E V Z Y W L J Z O M B I E
S T H E K A E S P Y L A C O P A
A C T I O N H O R R O R G T P X
B L C P P S U A N O O W K O E S
V N O I T C E F N I H J B H K R
```

ONE CUT OF THE DEAD (page 146)

```
Z K N Q X F X N N G C F M O B K
T R P K V T Q O P X J D I K L C
T Y T P Q J H I J A P A N E S E
F Z Y B I V I T V B L L N T L D
L F A U X R E A L I T Y F E R E
X S I N G L E T A K E U N T M N
W Y H M Q O D I A B P M G D A O
E H S H R H O P V F A L X F R D
R C A O Q A P A H H Z E D F G N
E V U R R N A J C C I T Y O C A A
I E G O O H I D O R T E R I N A
B S I R U B D V I U R N U K E R
M H H Y M W U S T A N I H C P P
O N O I S I V E L E T E V I L
Z W Z O M B I E C O M E D Y W W
```

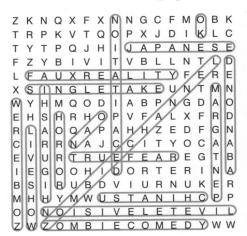

189

ANSWERS

HEREDITARY (page 148)

```
S G M Y O Q M M W Y M G V F Y T S P X N
T K J N S E I T Y L I M A F Q J F S N O I
U S P I R I T U A L A D V I S E R Y O I S
B M T R S V D F K P L H V F K S T C M S S
E P J F V O W E Y V C J C D X W G H I S E
D B S G O T H G T J C B C J C O R O A E S
L G L Z Z O S K B G A K V E L J A L P S S
A D A W A E T T E L L O C I N O T O G N I
I R N S U T H E G R A H A M S E W V C M O
R N O I A G O D E C A P I T A T I O N C K N
O T M R K C O H S C I T C A L Y H P A N A
C E T K E C P U I D I A O S R L Z L H R T
E D L S A L S E M V R R M V D Y I L C I I
R I L U T R A G I C A C C I D E N T Y T A
I V C H E R E D I T A R Y H A H H S N A O B T
M E O V A O C C U L T S I G I L S N E E
O X U D E L O P E N O H P E L E T A A R
Y L I M A F G N I V E I R G F Z W Y A W
```

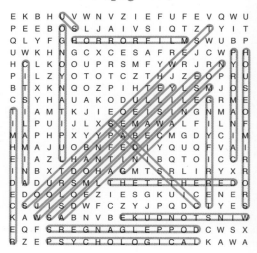

US (page 152)

```
E K B H U V W N V Z I E F U F E V Q W U
P E E B O S L J A I V S I Q T Z T Y I T
Q L Y F G H O R R O R F I L M S W U B P
U W K H K O O U P R S M F Y W R J R N Y O
P I L Z Y O T O T C Z T H J Z E O P R U
B T X K N Q O Z P I H T E Y L S M J O S
C S Y H A U A K O D U L L I L E G R M E
I L P U I J L X S E M A W A L F I L N F
M A P H P X Y Y P A B E C M G D Y C I M
H M A J U O B N F E D Y Q U Q F V A I I
I N B X T D O H A G M T S R L I R Y X R
D A D U R S M L T H E T E T H E R E D O
E D O O L O E Z I E S G K U I C E N E R
C S U I S D W F C Z Y J P Q D C T Y E S
K A W S A B N V B E K U D N O T S N I W
E Q F S R E G N A L P E P P O D C W S X
R Z E P S Y C H O L O G I C A L K A W A
```

A QUIET PLACE (page 150)

```
G M Q M U V K C E V E L Y N Z T
O S S N E I L A D N I L B P N S
S R I Z U Q N W N A G E R A M P
K E K L Q Q C D B E A U L G I S
E M S F E U S Y A J P P A H L K
G I N I Z N K P K P M U S H R R
U Y B A O E F W A I A L B I Y A
L R S C L E W P R L Q Y L R R
A U K O D L S S S N T P F E C I
L N N N H M Y M Z Z A H T E U E
N T H C W O O V V L F M W C S E
G I P O S T A P O C A L Y P T I C
I C J X X R O R R O H I F I C S
S N O I T C A R T S I D I H K K
```

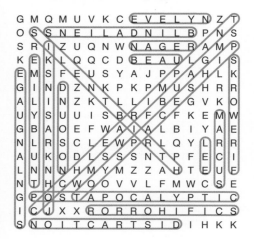

MIDSOMMAR (page 154)

```
Z A L P D M U R D E R D D Y J S
R U N E K G D A F L H B F H F D
H A L L U C I N O G E N I C R N
A K U L E W P H L N P Z I T N E
L N V E I P U S K U A O N V L D
S I N A D S K O H A G R E P K E
I A V U M G H J O P U S E U R W
N M C E C U L T R U N U G R A I
G F J R U T H X R T I D U A N O
L S A J I M U O S S E M Y A S F
A B H U O F R V R E M N A A S I B
N U Q I E G I V C T Z J M C I R C
D P V L O Q E C B T A M M U R H J
E N U M M O C L E A C T A Q F X
I M U S H R O O M S Y P R L X R
V U R E M M U S D I M E K I X S
```

ANSWERS

LITTLE MONSTERS (page 156)

```
K R D C P Y E Q Q Y U C I R H R
W O C P R V A C T I O N L W L A
O R H K A U W K Q Z H U N Q Y M
Y R T D B S I Z O P U O J S V Z
M O E C L T V J R E H C A E T F
B H D F T E N A I C I S U M N I
U Y D A P S O A Z R E M E F V U
B D Y R M T T E S S Z T Y B X S
X E D M F I E L D T R I P U R E
E M T Q X N L K X H F U P H H I
K O R R G G E I I X U B V A A B
O C W N A K F F T G E N A U Y M
W F U M P H V E A B Z C D J O
U E H Y V M A Z G L R Y E R V Z
C L N K H Z J L I U I Y D E C X
X C R L A C I S U M H X R Y N V
```

HIS HOUSE (page 160)

```
N S L I C L L B E F N I P X N J
O T Y U A E T H I E F J K S A N
S S E T M N X F J D B P N V D O
E O D I S N E T D G A O E L U M
S H I R I A D Y K W I P L S S L
N G Z I C H M A S S A C R E H S
E P C A A C Q J I G F V D F T Y
P Y Y U R B H F V N B G P U B U W
S I R Q A S S I M I L A T I O N
U G E K E I G N I T N U A H S I
S S F C U L T U R E S H O C K R
C V U B X G K O M T P J A T E U
T F G C D N T N E M R O T B E J
K L E G F E E S F H T E P A L E
Y D E T W D S Z U X L O N D O N
I B S U Q R T B B W V J R P R H
```

THE LIGHTHOUSE (page 158)

```
R Z U D O B C E X W F L E M E G
T I J N U V P S K K I H M N B A
L H S A H S A U I R E N A H G B
M A C L O E W O P K R S S F Z V
E F R G R I G H S M N Q J L W L
R C I N R P F T Y I K S J M O X
Z O M E O G Q H C V E U Q U Q W
S Y S W R L R G H G O R I R H P
P T H E S U L I O C S V W D Z M
E T A N I C U L L A H I I E O N
K E W E K A W W O R X V C R T H
K D M T E T J X G O W A K A M I
H Q R Z E Z H T I L F U I H F B
R E L L I R H T C Q Y C E N W F
D I A M R E M Y A L C Y I S T S
T A A L C O H O L I S M E R Y J
```

THE INVISIBLE MAN (page 162)

```
J E R X I D A G B C E V Z U F W
H S E M A J Y N X S E T N J Z U
D A P W P O P I M I S C V E U G
D R U G G E D T G D T I I U W R
E H H L Q E T H F V G N L L R I
F M K R P L K G R J Y V C F I P
B O L P A S W I A H P I L A N A
J T A B H L R L M I O S Z K G G
P R O P T I C S E N G I N E E R
T C E A Q T J A D Y C B S D N V
W W S Y E T T G M I Z L T D A U
Y B C U S H S K U S P E A E I Y
T P A U W R U N R M P Z L A R T
S E P V Y O I G D X B E K T D Y
K S E B U A T Y E Y V M E H A Z
F I Y Z G T F C B L H U D B T W
```

191

ANSWERS

PREY (page 164)

```
M K U R N X V Z W S T Z X J F R
S T O Z A M B K M U P I T S D G
A U A L R P I H S P O R D I Z I
R M F Q U U P B R E L A E H Z S
I Z P R E D A T O R C Q M K N V
I L O T S I P K C O L T N I L F
W W Y Q F Y T O M T N D A F L U
A D W I Y D B V I V O L Y X K R
R X V G H A I A A O P I L Z G T
C T A A B E B Q L T C I X M P R
H R N Z M P C B A Q O B Q U J A
I E V M H Z N E P A A K E K Q P
E T L O W E R B O D Y H E A T P
F N I W E G Z U H Z R R D F E E
Y U X R N H C E H C N A M O C R
W H G B X T M E V A Z V Z Z Z S
```

M3GAN (page 168)

```
Y S S E N E R A W A F L E S K L
N M U R D E R S U I C I D E O A
V S N B Y T L E V I L D O L L N
R E V I R D W E R C S T T Z E O
J G R B S U B Y E V P O S V R I
L T O E N Z C A D Y J B I R U T
N E R Y F G A E E L X O C X T O
V P R N R L R B A W F R I T P M
Y T O S H E C C D P M D I U A C
D D H W L W R G P Z K I O N K N
L E I Q Z T A G A O Y O B K I W
U I F W P H S E R G N N O I O I
H S I E F U H T E K E A R V I N
P G C X N X I J N I N M X U T G
C O S B V D H D T W V U M E O J
T S N U D H S W S C H J A M B
```

TALK TO ME (page 166)

```
R A P F Z B R Q M P L T N O H L
C N O I T C E N N O C X M K K N
S H X Z L F E J S S L E J J I
D P W U R O Y O C S X F E B A N
W S I M D N A H D E M L A B M E
V W M R X E E M U S Q R E R I T
T A M N I V Q E R S J A M M E Y
L X X T G T D H A I O A O B D S
R J A D E Z S C T O S I T J I E
F C Y R E T S Y M N S M K C A C
A Q J S T A B B I N G E L R L O
M U T I L A T E U D H C A U E N
K H E Z B H A Y L E Y K T T D D
O U E B A N I U O Y T E L I A S
Z Z O V E R T A K E N I E H O N
S D S A W Q A K H Z Y E L I R I
```

RENFIELD (page 170)

```
T B E W R P O E R E B E C C A N
E D P D A Q N C B E O B H D V E
D L E Y I N O I T C A W T M M P
E Z C L D T L D B G V Y U O U
Y I E N I O K O K C W B N U O R
L F H E M S U P E R S P E E D G
O N R D A M S T V A P R S S T O
B E N N F V E P F L Z I T N U T
O B T E Y J R U H U H W S M U R
S D J P V Z V R J C C Q R M O O
A C S E C N A R F A L L E B S P
J J N D H F N O S R B Q P S T A P
R W P O H Q T C Q D L L U T E U S
N S X C S E R I P M A V S E E
S R O R R O H Y D E M O C R H E
Y T I L A T R O M M I P Y S D T
```